Checkmate! Mateo

Fidel Monte

BMN Publishing

Contents

Prologue

Two years had passed since Mateo stood at the podium as valedictorian, his voice steady and full of promise. The memory of applause still lived faintly in his mind, like a fading echo from another lifetime. Back then, he believed excellence and perseverance would finally win him peace. He believed recognition would silence the doubts, and faithfulness would shield him from unseen enemies.

But the seminary had its own designs.

By his second year in theology, whispers began to move through the corridors — whispers he could neither trace nor silence. He noticed how some formators avoided his eyes, how conversations hushed when he entered a room. He carried on with his duties, as always, with precision and grace, yet beneath the surface something had already been decided.

One late afternoon, Mateo was called into the rector's office. The air inside was heavy, not with anger, but with something far colder — resignation. He was told to leave. No explanation. No crime named. No failure is cited. Just a verdict, delivered as if rehearsed long before he had ever walked into the theology department.

For a moment, he could not speak. The words fell upon him like a sentence from a judge, stripping him not only of his place but also of the future he had devoted his entire youth to pursuing.

Mateo left the office quietly, the echo of his footsteps against the old seminary floor sounding louder than ever before. His hands trembled, but his mind burned with a single, unrelenting question: *Was this truly the will of God, or the work of men who had conspired against him?*

The chessboard of his life had shifted. Every move he had made with care, every sacrifice, every hour of prayer and study—all of it seemed to collapse into one cruel declaration: *Checkmate.*

Yet Mateo knew one thing with certainty. The game was not yet over.

This was not the end of his story.

This was only the beginning of *Checkmate! Mateo.*

CHAPTER I

The Prefect's Garden

The theology seminary was a world of its own, set apart not only by its academic rigor but also by the curious personalities that ruled its daily rhythms. Each priest-professor had his peculiarities, his little obsessions, and his unique way of leaving a mark on the seminarians under his care. Mateo, newly arrived from philosophy, could not help but notice these eccentricities—and before long, his own gifts became entangled in their interests.

Foremost among them was the Prefect. To new-comers, he seemed almost contradictory in his pursuits. In the mornings, he could be found pruning and watering his miniature trees in the small garden he had cultivated between the two wings of the theology building. Rows of bonsai stood neatly on their pedestals, alongside flowering shrubs that burst with colors unusual in such a cloistered environment. The Prefect moved among them with quiet devotion, his thick hands surprisingly gentle as he trimmed a branch or repositioned a pot to catch the sunlight just right.

Yet those same hands bore the calluses of a body-builder. His afternoons were often spent in a modest gym tucked away in one of the unused storage rooms, where he lifted iron bars with a focus that mirrored his gardening. His physique was firm, his movements deliberate, as if sculpting not just his plants but himself. The seminarians whispered about it, half in jest, half in admiration: *the man of flowers and muscles.*

It was only a matter of time before he took an interest in Mateo.

The Prefect had observed the young seminarian during community chores and liturgical activities. Mateo's discipline, his eye for detail, and his calm patience with others stood out. And so, little by little, Mateo found himself summoned to the garden—not as a guest, but as an assistant.

"Hold this pot steady, Aragon," the Prefect would say, adjusting the roots with surgical precision. "Fetch me the smaller shears."

"Do you see this branch? It bends the wrong way. Clip it, but carefully."

At first, Mateo welcomed the invitations. He loved the quiet of the garden, the way the fragrance of damp soil mingled with the faint rustle of leaves in the breeze. It reminded him of his childhood afternoons in the province, where life moved with the rhythm of the earth. Here, in theology, the garden seemed almost a refuge.

But as the weeks passed, he noticed something more subtle: his presence was no longer a matter of occasional help. He was expected. Whether he had an exam to prepare for, choir rehearsals to manage, or community duties to attend, the Prefect assumed that Mateo would appear whenever a new pot arrived, whenever the hedges grew wild, or whenever the bonsai demanded trimming.

The garden became another classroom for Mateo—one not listed in the curriculum, but no less demanding. He learned the art of balance, how every cut mattered, and how restraint often achieved more than excess. The Prefect would sometimes pause in his work and remark in a low, almost philosophical tone:

"Life is like these trees, Aragon. You shape it slowly, patiently. You must see what it is meant to become and remove what gets in the way. Do it wrong, and you kill the tree. Do it right, and it flourishes."

Mateo nodded respectfully, though in his heart he wondered if the words carried another meaning, one directed more toward him than the bonsai.

For now, he obeyed without complaint. After all, he was new to the theology department of the diocesan seminary, eager to prove himself and show that he could be of service. Yet already, in the quiet trimming of branches, a pattern was forming: his gifts, his discipline, and his availability were being noticed—and claimed.

Little did he know that the garden was only the beginning. Each priest-teacher in theology would soon seek a piece of him, each in his own way, until Mateo's life felt less like a flowering tree and more like one being pruned on all sides at once.

CHAPTER 2

The Master of Chants

If the Prefect claimed Mateo for the garden, then Father Anselmo—the Liturgy professor—soon discovered him for the chapel.

Father Anselmo was not a man of flowers or weights. His passion was sound, pure, and ancient. He believed that the liturgy was not merely prayed but sung, that every psalm, every chant, every intonation carried within it the rhythm of heaven itself. He walked with a quiet dignity, his head often tilted as if listening to something only he could hear, and when he spoke in class, his voice rolled like low thunder in the mountains.

It happened during an ordinary evening prayer. The seminarians gathered in the chapel, their voices blending in the simple tones of Gregorian chant. Mateo, seated among the others, let his voice rise with the rest—steady, warm, unforced. He did not notice that Father Anselmo, sitting at the back, had opened his eyes and fixed them on him.

The next day, a message arrived: *"Aragon, see me in the sacristy after supper."*

Mateo obeyed. He found the professor arranging hymnals and smoothing out the old, wrinkled covers of chant books.

"Sing for me," Father Anselmo said without preamble.

"Father?" Mateo hesitated.

"Sing. The *Ave Maris Stella.*"

So he did. His voice filled the quiet sacristy, untrained but instinctively graceful, carrying the solemn Latin melody with clarity. Father Anselmo closed his eyes, nodding slightly with each phrase. When Mateo finished, the old priest spoke:

"You will lead the chants. From now on. Every Vespers, every Lauds, every solemn liturgy."

And so it began.

Mateo was thrust into the role of *cantor*, the guiding voice of the community's prayer. He spent hours with Father Anselmo, learning the delicate art of breathing between phrases, the subtle rise and fall that carried centuries of tradition. The professor demanded excellence, but he also trusted Mateo in a way that startled the young seminarian. He would leave him alone with the choir, expecting him to correct his mistakes and shape the rhythm of prayer itself.

At first, Mateo was proud. To guide the community in chant was no small honor. His classmates respected him; some even admired him. But pride soon gave way to pressure. Every note had to be perfect. Every entrance, every cadence. If a brother slipped, all eyes turned to Mateo, as though the fault were his.

Worse, his other tasks did not vanish. The Prefect still expected him in the garden. His professors still demanded essays and readings. His classmates sought his help in philosophy debates and in music rehearsals. Mateo's days began to stretch thin, and the quiet nights of restlessness returned.

Father Anselmo, however, remained unyielding. "The liturgy," he reminded him, "is the Church's highest act. You must give it everything. If you fail here, you fail everywhere."

The words cut deep. Mateo nodded, but in his heart he wondered, *"How much of me is left to give?"*

Still, he obeyed. The chapel echoed with his voice, the prayers lifted on his melody, and Father Anselmo looked on with satisfaction. The seminary began to call him *the master of chants*—a title he never asked for, but one that chained him more firmly to the service of others.

By now, two parts of his life had been claimed: the garden and the chapel. Yet more awaited. The theology seminary was filled with men who recognized not only his devotion but also the various aspects of his talent. Each, in turn, would want a piece of Mateo Aragon.

Chapter 3

The Rhetorician's Apprentice

The theology seminary was not only a place of prayer and discipline; it was a crucible of words. Words were debated, preached, written on parchment, and spoken from pulpits. And no one embodied that more than Father Benedicto, the professor of Dogmatic Theology.

Father Benedicto possessed a sharp intellect. His lectures were precise, his arguments airtight, and his quotations from Church Fathers and philosophers rattled off with the ease of memory. Yet beneath his calm tone lay a subtle fire. He did not merely teach doctrine—he wielded it, testing his students in public debates that left many stammering.

It was during one of these sessions that Mateo first caught his attention.

The class was tasked with defending or refuting the statement, *"Grace cannot be resisted if it is truly divine."* The debate grew messy; seminarians stumbled, citing Thomas Aquinas incorrectly or collapsing under Augustine's paradoxes. Finally, Father Benedicto pointed at Mateo.

"Aragon. Stand. Let us hear you."

Mateo's heart raced. He had not prepared to be called that day. Yet he rose, smoothed the crease of his cassock, and began to speak. At first, his words were halting, but as he leaned into the reasoning, something awoke in him. He drew from memory—not just theology texts, but fragments of philosophy, Scripture, and even a line from Kahlil Gibran he once pondered during his philosophy years. He wove them together carefully, like a melody building toward resolution.

When he finished, silence hung in the classroom. Then, slowly, Father Benedicto smiled—not a warm smile, but the sharp one of recognition, like a chess master meeting an unexpected opponent.

"Very well, Aragon," he said. "From now on, you will help me prepare disputations. You have a mind that can carry words to their sharpest point."

And thus Mateo found himself drawn into another orbit.

Evenings that might have been spent studying in solitude were now given to drafting arguments, revising essays, and crafting speeches that Father Benedicto would deliver at diocesan conferences. Mateo immersed himself in the realm of ideas, crafting words he had never publicly spoken.

The work stretched him thin. His fingers were stained with ink, and the glow of oil lamps in the library shortened his nights. Yet he found a strange satisfaction in it. For when words flowed rightly, they sang in his mind like music. Sometimes, as he wrote, he almost forgot the weight pressing on him—the garden duties, the chants, the sleepless nights of questioning.

But satisfaction came with a cost. His classmates began to notice the favoritism. Whispers rose that Mateo was Father Benedicto's chosen apprentice, groomed for academic glory. Some admired him; others envied him. And Mateo, caught in the center, felt the net tightening.

In quiet moments he asked himself, *"Am I becoming a priest of prayer, or merely a servant of men's ambitions?"*

Still, he pressed on. He owed obedience. He owed effort. And he owed it to himself to prove that his mind, like his voice and his hands, was a gift not wasted.

Three priests now pulled at him: the Prefect of the garden, the Master of Chants, and the Rhetorician. Each demanded a different part of him. Mateo gave, and gave, and gave—until he wondered what part of himself remained unclaimed.

CHAPTER 4

The Music Beyond the Walls

The seminary days were long, and yet the weeks seemed to blur together. Mateo was already stretched between the Prefect's garden, Father Anselmo's chant rehearsals, and Father Benedicto's disputations. He sometimes wondered if there would be anything left of him if each priest kept claiming a piece.

Then Father Chris came along.

Father Chris was different from the others. He was younger than most of the faculty, energetic, with a ready laugh and an ease of manner that disarmed the seminarians. While the others carried the weight of authority like an invisible robe, Father Chris carried it lightly, as though priesthood were not only a calling but also a kind of companionship.

One afternoon, after a pastoral lecture, Father Chris motioned for Mateo to stay behind.

"Mateo, I've been watching you," he began, his tone casual but intent. "You've a way with music—not just performing, but teaching it. You bring order out of voices. You make people want to sing."

Mateo felt his chest tighten with both pride and unease. Compliments often carried hidden burdens in the seminary.

"I teach part-time at St. Raphael's College nearby," Father Chris continued. "They've asked me to prepare the students for their Christmas program. But my schedule is already impossible. I was wondering…" He leaned forward slightly. "Would you come with me once a week? It would only take two hours. Help me train them in their songs."

The request startled Mateo. No other priest had asked him to serve beyond the seminary walls. The idea of stepping into another campus, meeting new students, and guiding them—something in it felt like freedom.

"I'd be honored, Father," Mateo replied softly.
And so it began.
After finishing his seminary classes every Wednesday afternoon, Mateo would ride with Father Chris

to St. Raphael's. The campus was livelier, younger, and filled with laughter and the chatter of students who were not burdened with cassocks or formational rules. The first time Mateo entered the music hall, he was greeted by rows of eager faces—teenagers with bright eyes and untamed energy, holding song sheets in their hands.

At first, the students were shy around him. He was, after all, "the seminarian from the major seminary." But soon, as he guided them with patience—teaching them how to breathe, how to hold a note, and how to listen to each other's voices—they warmed to him. His way of teaching was firm yet gentle. He corrected without shaming and encouraged without overpraising.

Week after week, their sound grew stronger and more confident. By December, when the Christmas program came, their carols filled the hall with such harmony that even the college dean congratulated Father Chris.

Of course, Father Chris did not take the credit. He nudged Mateo forward. "This is the man you should thank. He's the one who shaped your students' voices."

The students clapped for Mateo, and for the first time in years, he felt not just useful but celebrated outside the seminary walls.

That Christmas marked the beginning of a deeper bond between Mateo and Father Chris. Their Wednesday trips became more than just rehearsals. On the road, they talked. Sometimes about pastoral work, sometimes about music, sometimes about life itself. Father Chris had a way of asking questions that felt less like interrogation and more like companionship.

"Do you ever wonder," he asked once, as they sat in a small café after rehearsal, "whether God calls us to priesthood for what we can give or for what we must endure?"

Mateo smiled faintly. "Every day."

Father Chris chuckled. "Then you're in good company."

Those conversations stayed with Mateo. They reminded him that formation was not only about rules, duties, or surviving the weight of expectations. It could also be about friendship—something he had not felt in a long while with any of his superiors.

As the academic year pressed on, Father Chris once again enlisted his help—this time for the college's graduation ceremony. The program required solemn hymns, a farewell song, and even a piece to accompany the march of graduates. Mateo threw himself into the work. By now, the students adored him. They greeted him like a mentor, teased him like an older brother, and trusted him to lead them in music that would crown their school year.

The graduation performance turned out splendid. Parents, faculty, and guests spoke of how the music elevated the entire event. And again, Father Chris made sure Mateo was recognized, whispering to colleagues, "This young man will go far."

For Mateo, it was not only an honor—it was nourishment for a soul often drained by suspicion, envy, or the cold politics of seminary life.

Back in the seminary, however, his new role did not go unnoticed. Some fellow seminarians whispered about his "special privileges" with Father Chris. Others grumbled that he was being groomed for something beyond their reach. Mateo heard the rumors but kept silent. He had learned caution long ago.

Still, he carried himself with dignity. His duties inside the seminary remained impeccable. He fulfilled his work in the garden, the choir, and the disputations. And yet, every Wednesday, he stepped into another world—a world where music built bridges, where students looked up to him, and where a priest treated him not as a pawn but as a partner.

It gave him hope that perhaps, even amid the storm of expectations and the quiet undercurrent of envy, he could find spaces where his gifts were not exploited but valued.

He hoped that maybe, just maybe, God was weaving all these scattered threads—gardens, chants, words, and now this music beyond the walls—into a tapestry with a purpose he could not yet see.

CHAPTER 5

The Weight of Leadership

The first semester of theology had barely settled when Mateo found himself summoned to the Rector's office. Father Michael, the seminary rector, was not a man one could easily read. His words were kind, but his eyes carried calculation, as if each decision he made was part of a larger design.

"Come in, Mateo," he said, gesturing for him to sit. The Rector's office was neatly arranged, its bookshelves lined with thick tomes of theology, canon law, and philosophy. A crucifix hung prominently above his desk, illuminated by the afternoon sun.

Mateo sat quietly, uncertain why he had been called.

"Mateo," Father Michael began, folding his hands on the desk, "I've been observing you. You are not only gifted in music but also in discipline, diligence, and character. The community looks up to you. Even in your first year here, you have earned their respect."

Mateo lowered his eyes slightly, unsure how to respond. Compliments in the seminary often came with expectations.

The Rector leaned forward. "I want you to consider running for president of the entire theology student body."

Mateo's breath caught. He had not expected this. "Father Rector," he began carefully, "I am honored by your trust. But I am only in my first year of studies. There are seniors here, men with more experience and more maturity. Wouldn't it be presumptuous of me?"

Father Michael shook his head slowly, smiling faintly. "That is precisely why you should run. The presidency is not about age, Mateo. It is about vision, integrity, and leadership. The student body needs a leader who can inspire, not merely someone who has been here longer. You are that man."

Mateo hesitated. He could feel the weight of the request pressing on him. Already, his weeks were full: assisting in music, teaching at St. Raphael's, helping the Prefect, excelling in academics. To add leadership for the entire theology department seemed almost too much.

Sensing his reluctance, Father Michael continued, "Listen to me, Mateo. This is not only about this year. Leadership here is training for the greater responsibilities ahead. Imagine yourself, a priest someday—not only a servant of the altar, but a guide to others, a formator, and maybe even a rector yourself one day. These experiences shape the priest you will become. This is preparation for the ministry God is entrusting to you."

The words lingered in the air. Rector. Professor. Guide. They were titles Mateo had never dared to imagine for himself. To be considered worthy of such a path both flattered and terrified him.

"But Father Rector," Mateo said softly, "what if I fail? What if I am not ready?"

Father Michael's smile deepened, not unkind but firm. "That is the language of fear, Mateo. And fear is not of God. You have all the qualities needed. You only need to trust that what God has begun in you, He will complete. Let the rest take care of itself."

Mateo sat in silence. His heart was divided. He longed for a simple seminary life—prayer, study, music, and the slow shaping of the soul. At every juncture, someone perceived in him a deeper potential, something more worthy of exploration, demand, and public display.

Finally, he gave a slow nod. "If you believe this is what God wants through you, Father, then I will try."

The Rector's eyes glimmered with quiet satisfaction. "Good. Prepare yourself. Elections are coming soon. And Mateo—remember, leadership is not a burden if it is embraced as service."

That night, as Mateo knelt in the chapel, the echo of the Rector's words filled his mind. Service. Leadership. Vision. Yet in the stillness, he whispered his own plea to God:

"Lord, give me strength not to lose myself in the expectations of men. Help me remember who I am in You."

The flickering sanctuary lamp was his only answer, but it was enough.

Mateo rose, knowing that a new chapter of his seminary life was about to unfold—not one he had chosen, but one that was now entrusted to him.

CHAPTER 6

The Election

The announcement came during Monday's general assembly. The auditorium was filled with seminarians from every year level, their black cassocks forming a sea of uniformity. Yet beneath the calm exterior was a charged energy: election season always stirred both competition and quiet anxiety.

Father Michael stepped up to the podium. His voice, steady and commanding, carried across the hall.

"Brothers, as you know, it is once again time to choose your new set of student officers. Leadership is not about power but service. Remember these words as you consider your vote."

The floor buzzed with low chatter as names of potential candidates floated in the air. Third-years spoke of their blockmates who had been waiting for this opportunity. Fourth-years were confident one of their own would win, as tradition often dictated.

But then, the whispers grew sharper. "They say Mateo is running."

Heads turned toward him, sitting quietly in the second row. He felt the weight of their stares. Some carried respect. Others, suspicion. A few even disapproval.

"First-year?" someone muttered. "Impossible."
"He's too new."
"But you can't deny—he's got a following already."
"Because of music. But politics is different."

Mateo remained still, his hands clasped tightly. He had no grand speeches, no posters, and no promises. The Rector's words echoed in his memory: *Leadership is service.*

When the time for campaign speeches arrived, the senior candidates strode confidently to the podium, one after another. They spoke of programs, reforms, discipline, and tradition. Their words were polished and rehearsed. Applause followed, measured and polite.

Then it was Mateo's turn.

He walked slowly to the front, his cassock brushing against the wooden steps. As he reached the microphone, the hall seemed to grow tense, expectant.

"I have no long speech to give," he began quietly. His voice carried a calm strength, not loud but steady. "I am only in my first year here. Many of you have more experience than I do. I cannot promise great reforms or extraordinary plans. What I can promise is this: if you choose me, I will listen. I will serve. I will stand with you, not above you. My only desire is to help us all become the priests God is calling us to be."

A pause followed. The simplicity of his words seemed almost out of place amid the grand declarations of the others. Yet something in his sincerity cut through the noise.

"I ask nothing for myself," Mateo concluded, "only that we walk this path together as brothers. Whatever happens today, may God's will be done."

He stepped down. Silence lingered for a moment before a wave of applause broke out—stronger and more genuine than before. Not everyone clapped, but enough did for Mateo to feel the stirring of something he had not expected: hope.

The voting took place immediately. The ballots were counted under the watchful eyes of faculty. Mateo sat in the chapel during the tally, whispering a prayer. He did not crave victory, but he prayed for peace—peace with whatever result came.

When the final numbers were announced, a murmur swept through the auditorium. Against all predictions, Mateo had won. Although it was by a narrow margin, Mateo's victory was sufficient to make him the new president of the theology department.

Father Michael, watching from the side, allowed himself the faintest smile. The others—some stunned, some resentful—looked at Mateo with fresh eyes.

For his part, Mateo bowed his head. "Thank you, brothers," he said simply. "Let us begin."

That night, alone in his room, he wrote in his journal:

Lord, why do You keep putting me in places I never ask for? You know my heart longs for silence, not the stage. Yet here I am again. If this is Your will, then grant me the grace not to seek honor but to serve in humility. And when my strength falters, remind me that Yours is enough.

The lamp flickered, casting shadows on the page. Another unexpected chapter in Mateo's journey had begun.

CHAPTER 7

The Shadows of Rumor

Mateo had barely settled into his new role when resistance began to surface. On the surface, life at the theology department moved on as expected. He chaired meetings, organized schedules, and listened to the concerns of seminarians with the same patience that marked his earlier leadership in music. His presence at the head table during assemblies felt almost surreal, as if he had been lifted into a place he never sought.

But beneath the calm surface, whispers started to spread.

It began with two fourth-year seminarians who had long assumed the presidency would be theirs. Losing to a first-year had wounded their pride, and they would not let it rest. Over cups of coffee in the refectory and hushed conversations in corridors, they began to plant seeds of suspicion.

"Have you noticed how Mateo always disappears after meetings?" one said.

"Exactly," the other agreed. "And he's from the northern part of San Agustin, isn't he? Some of those towns have a history with the leftists."

"You're right. Imagine if he's been attending meetings with rebels all along."

The rumor was absurd, but in a closed community like the seminary, absurdities could take root quickly. Soon, whispers followed Mateo wherever he went. In the library, heads turned as he walked past. In the garden, conversations fell silent at his approach. Some seminarians looked at him with quiet doubt; others avoided him altogether.

Mateo noticed the change but could not understand it. *Why are they looking at me that way?* he wondered. Still, he pressed on with his duties, unaware that a slow fire of sabotage was spreading behind him.

Meanwhile, Mateo's leadership was beginning to show fruit. He organized a weekly forum where seminarians could voice their concerns directly to faculty representatives. He encouraged the less confident brothers to take part in choir rehearsals, reminding them that music was not just performance but prayer. His sincerity won many hearts, and for some, his generosity only deepened their admiration.

But for the few who had plotted against him, admiration was dangerous. They doubled their efforts, claiming that Mateo's sudden rise in influence was "political," that he was using the seminary as a steppingstone for a bigger agenda.

Their most damaging claim was whispered during a late-night recreation: "Do you know Mateo was seen talking to strangers outside the seminary walls? They were organizers from the leftist movement. He's not just a seminarian—he's a rebel sympathizer."

The accusation, unfounded as it was, traveled fast. By morning, it had reached the ears of the more cautious faculty members. Concerned glances were exchanged during staff meetings. Some wondered aloud whether Mateo's influence was becoming "too strong, too quickly."

Mateo, meanwhile, kept his focus on the responsibilities given to him. He prepared reports, organized events, and balanced his studies with precision. His professors praised his academic performance, and Father Chris continued to encourage his musical involvement.

Yet, at night, alone in his room, Mateo began to feel the weight of something unseen. His prayers grew heavier, his words more desperate:

Lord, why do I feel surrounded, even though no one speaks? Why does silence carry sharp edges? If this is another test, grant me the grace to endure it without bitterness.

He did not yet know the depth of the plot against him, nor how close the rumor was to threatening his place in the seminary itself.

But the shadows were moving, slowly, deliberately.

And soon, they would step into the light.

CHAPTER 8

Under the Rector's Eyes

The seminary bell rang for morning prayers, its solemn chime echoing through the narrow halls. Mateo rose, washed his face, and dressed in silence. His life followed the rhythm of the seminary clock, yet a subtle heaviness had begun to follow him everywhere he went. It wasn't the kind of heaviness that came from fatigue or study; it was the weight of unseen eyes, of whispers that brushed past him like cold drafts in the chapel.

Mateo told himself it was his imagination, but deep down he knew something was wrong.

The first to feel the effect of the rumors was Father Prefect. While tending to his bonsai garden one afternoon, two older seminarians approached him casually. Their tone was deliberately light, but their words were sharp.

"Father, we've noticed Mateo often slips out after meetings," one said, trimming his fingernails with exaggerated care.

The other chimed in, "Yes, and some of us wonder if he might be… distracted by activities outside. Perhaps political ones."

Father Prefect raised an eyebrow. "Political?" he repeated, his voice calm, but his eyes narrowing.

"Some say he has connections with leftist groups," the seminarian said quickly, as though it were simply a passing thought. "We don't know if it's true, of course. But in times like these, can we really be too careful?"

They left Father Prefect with that poisonous seed. By evening, it had taken root in his mind, and by the next morning, it was quietly passed along during a faculty meeting.

Father Michael, the Rector, listened in silence as Father Prefect shared the concern. Around the long wooden table, some faculty members looked uneasy. Others dismissed it as gossip. But Father Michael did not speak; he only pressed his hands together and leaned back in his chair.

He knew Mateo's reputation: disciplined, talented, obedient, and unusually gifted for his age. But he also understood how the mere hint of political entanglement could shake institutions like theirs. If the rumor spread beyond the seminary walls, even unfounded, it could damage not only Mateo but also the institution itself.

That evening, after compline prayers, Father Michael stood by his window overlooking the campus. He thought of Mateo—his steady leadership, his musical brilliance, and his evident faith. Could such a young man harbor a secret so dark? Or was he merely the victim of envy?

Father Michael decided then: he would watch Mateo closely. Not openly, but silently, like a shepherd observing a stray lamb to see if it wandered by choice or by accident.

Mateo, oblivious to the depth of suspicion, continued his work with quiet diligence. As student body president, he prepared for an inter-seminary dialogue where students from different religious houses would gather. He stayed up late polishing reports, balancing his schedule, and rehearsing choir pieces for Father Chris's college students.

His diligence only made the whispers sharper. *"Too perfect, too polished,"* some muttered. *"That kind of ambition hides something."*

One evening, as Mateo left the library, he passed by Father Michael in the corridor. The Rector greeted him warmly, as always, but there was something different in his gaze—an extra moment of scrutiny, as if he were measuring not just Mateo's words but his very breath.

"How are your studies progressing, Mateo?" Father Michael asked.

"They're going well, Father Rector," Mateo replied respectfully, lowering his eyes. "I've been preparing for the dialogue next week and finishing my papers for Philosophy of Religion."

"Good," Father Michael said softly. Then, after a pause, he added, "And outside of your duties? You haven't been… too distracted, I hope?"

Mateo blinked, startled. "No, Father. Not at all. I've given myself entirely to the seminary's work."

Father Michael nodded but said nothing more. He let the silence linger before walking past, leaving Mateo unsettled.

In the refectory, Mateo noticed more glances than before. At choir practice, some seminarians hesitated when he assigned parts, as if questioning his authority. Even Nick, his closest ally, seemed restless, though they refused to explain why.

One night, as he lay awake staring at the ceiling, Mateo whispered to himself:

Lord, why do I feel judged for things I have not done? Why do shadows grow even when I walk in Your light?

He remembered the threats of Fr. Alvarez, the manipulations of Miss Lolita, and the cruel telegram that almost ruined him. Was this another test? Or was this the beginning of his undoing?

Father Michael's silent watchfulness grew over the weeks. He observed Mateo in prayer, at meetings, and in classes. He spoke quietly to professors, asking for their impressions. Some praised Mateo's brilliance; others admitted they felt uneasy about how much influence he had gained so quickly.

At last, Father Michael knew he could not remain passive. He summoned Mateo to his office one afternoon, the heavy wooden door closing behind them with a thud.

"Mateo," the Rector began, his tone calm but firm. "I've heard things—things I wish I hadn't. I want to speak to you directly, not as a judge, but as a father concerned for his son."

Mateo's heart pounded. "What things, Father?"

Father Michael leaned forward, his eyes sharp but sorrowful. "There are whispers, Mateo. Whispers that you are involved with groups outside the seminary—groups opposed to the government. Some are saying you've attended their meetings."

The words struck Mateo like a blow. His mouth went dry, and for a moment, he could not breathe.

"Father, that is not true," Mateo said finally, his voice trembling but steady. "I have never met with such groups, nor do I have any desire to. My life is here, in the seminary. You know this."

"I want to believe you," Father Michael said softly. "And in truth, I do. But rumors, once sown, can be as dangerous as weeds in a garden. Even if false, they can strangle a vocation."

Mateo lowered his head, sorrow heavy in his chest. "Then what should I do, Father?"

Father Michael did not answer immediately. He walked to the window, hands clasped behind his back, gazing out at the setting sun.

"You will do what you have always done," he said at last. "Remain faithful. Excel in your duties. Do not give them reason to doubt. Time will reveal the truth, Mateo. But until then, I will be watching—not to condemn you, but to protect you."

Mateo felt both comforted and unsettled. He had the Rector's trust, but also his scrutiny. He was no longer just another seminarian; he was under the eye of the shepherd.

As Mateo left the office, his steps echoed down the hallway. The shadows of rumor had not destroyed him—but they had begun to shape his path in ways he could not yet see.

CHAPTER 9

Secrets Too Heavy

The week after Father Michael's private warning, Mateo worked harder than ever. He rose earlier, prayed longer, and spoke less. He poured his energy into his responsibilities—lectures, reports, and above all, the weekly music practices at St. Raphael College with Father Chris and his students. It was, in many ways, his escape.

The college students loved him. His patient teaching, his ability to draw music out of hesitant voices, and his calm authority—it earned him respect quickly. Father Chris would often beam proudly as Mateo conducted the choir, watching the young seminarians and students alike follow his lead with discipline and joy.

It was during one of those ordinary practices, in the middle of December preparations, that the secret fell upon Mateo like a stone.

They had just finished rehearsing *Angels We Have Heard on High*. The students laughed, some clapping at their own mistakes, while others stretched and reached for their cups of coffee and bread. Mateo joined them, grateful for a short break.

A young woman, quiet and soft-spoken, approached him. She carried her cup of coffee carefully, her eyes darting nervously toward the corner where Father Chris stood, chatting with another group.

"Brother Mateo," she whispered.

"Yes?" he answered, turning to her with his usual kindness.

She lowered her gaze, her hands trembling slightly. "I… I don't know who else to talk to. I need your help."

Mateo's brows furrowed. "What is it?"

The girl hesitated, her lips pressed tightly together. Then, as though the words had forced themselves out, she said:

"I'm in a relationship with Father Chris."

The world seemed to tilt. Mateo stared at her, his breath caught. Surely, he had misheard.

She continued, her voice breaking: "It's wrong, I know. I want it to end, but I don't know how. He says he loves me, but I feel trapped. Please, Brother Mateo... can you please help me?"

Mateo's throat tightened. A thousand thoughts rushed through his mind—shock, anger, and confusion. He looked over at Father Chris, still laughing with students, his jovial face betraying nothing.

"I..." Mateo faltered. "I'm sorry for what you're going through. But this is something... I cannot help you with."

Her eyes filled with tears, but she nodded, as if she had expected no other answer.

"I see," she whispered, before retreating to her seat.

Mateo placed his untouched coffee on the table. His hands shook as he returned to the piano, summoning the students for the second half of rehearsal. He forced his voice steady and forced his hands to play. But inside, he was crumbling.

That night, after supper at the seminary, Mateo sat alone in the library, trying to lose himself in his notes. His mind replayed the girl's words endlessly. He had kept his silence, but guilt pressed on him like a millstone.

The door creaked. Father Chris entered, his face set, his steps quick. He closed the door behind him and approached Mateo's table.

"Mateo," he said quietly, though his voice trembled. "We need to talk."

Mateo looked up, his chest tightening. "Yes, Father."

Father Chris pulled out a chair and sat opposite him, leaning forward. His face was a mixture of shame and desperation.

"I know what happened today," he began. "She spoke to you, didn't she?"

Mateo said nothing, but his silence was answer enough.

Father Chris rubbed his forehead with his hand. "You must understand... I never meant for it to happen. I was lonely. I thought I could guide her, but... it went further. Too far."

He swallowed hard. "I care for her, but I know it cannot last. It was a mistake. A terrible mistake."

Mateo lowered his eyes. He felt the weight of a priest's broken vow pressing onto his own shoulders.

"Father," Mateo said carefully, "this is not something I can carry for you. This is between you, God, and..." He hesitated. "...and the Church."

"I know," Father Chris whispered. Then, with sudden urgency, he reached across the table. "But you must promise me, Mateo—you must never speak of this incident to anyone. If the truth gets out, it will ruin me. Everything I've worked for will be gone. Do you understand?"

Mateo looked into his pleading eyes. The desperation was almost unbearable. He nodded slowly. "Your secret is safe with me, Father."

Father Chris exhaled, relief flooding his face. He patted Mateo's arm. "Thank you. I knew I could trust you. You're a good man, Mateo."

But when Father Chris left, Mateo remained at the table, staring blankly at his books. His soul was in turmoil. He had carried many burdens in the seminary—his own trials, his own enemies. But this was different. This was not his sin, yet it had been laid upon him to keep.

He whispered in the silence:

Lord, why do You let me see what I cannot unsee and hear what I cannot unhear? How can I carry secrets that are not mine to bear?

No answer came, only the distant toll of the bell. And once again, Mateo felt the shadows around him deepen.

CHAPTER 10

The Seeds of Distrust

The semester rolled on with its usual weight of assignments, recollections, and liturgical obligations. Mateo managed to steady himself after his unsettling conversation with Father Chris in the library. He told himself that silence was his only shield, that if he simply minded his own work, the secret would fade into the background of his already burdened conscience.

But silence, Mateo was learning, did not erase a wound.

It happened on an ordinary afternoon at St. Raphael College, only a week before the Christmas program. The choir had just completed a stirring rehearsal of the finale number. Father Chris had stepped outside to take a phone call, leaving Mateo to dismiss the students for a short break.

As Mateo lingered near the piano, wiping his forehead with a handkerchief, the young woman approached again. This time her face bore none of the restraint of their first encounter. Her cheeks were red, and her eyes glistened with tears. She carried no coffee cup, no mask of casualness—only raw desperation.

"Brother Mateo," she whispered, her voice shaking. "Please… I can't do this anymore. He won't let me go. I don't know what to do."

She clutched his sleeve, her grip trembling. Mateo looked around nervously, but the room was nearly empty, the other students busy outside in the corridor.

"Please," she pressed, her voice breaking into sobs. "You're the only one I can turn to. Tell me what to do. Help me—please."

She held his hands now, tightly, almost as if anchoring herself to him. Her knees bent slightly, and for a moment, Mateo feared she would collapse right there on the floor.

His heart pounded. He wanted to pull away, to retreat into the safety of silence again, but her eyes searched his with a desperation that tore at him.

"I'm sorry," Mateo said gently but firmly, his words deliberate. "I cannot interfere. I cannot be the one to untangle this. This matter is between you and him. I wish I could do more—but I cannot."

The girl's tears spilled freely now. She whispered something—*"I just want to be free"*—and let go of his hands at last, retreating toward the far corner, her body shaking with sobs.

Mateo sat down heavily at the piano bench, burying his face in his hands. *Lord, why me? Why place me here, caught in the middle of this?*

At that exact moment, Father Chris re-entered the rehearsal hall. His eyes immediately caught the sight of his student weeping in the corner and Mateo seated with his hands still half-raised from the encounter. He froze. His gaze dropped to Mateo's hands, then to the girl, and back again.

From where he stood, the picture was damning: his young student, holding Mateo's hands, weeping before him, almost kneeling. The interpretation took root instantly, and with it, a sharp stab of jealousy.

A shadow passed over Father Chris' face.

He said nothing during the rest of the rehearsal, though his voice was clipped and his instructions uncharacteristically curt. Mateo, unaware of what exactly Father Chris had seen, carried on quietly, sensing only a strange coldness in the air.

That evening, back at the seminary, Father Chris avoided Mateo altogether. Days turned into weeks, and their once warm camaraderie cooled into something formal, even distant. Where there had been trust, there was now suspicion. Where there had been laughter, there was now silence.

Mateo felt the change keenly. He had once counted Father Chris a friend, even a mentor. Now he saw only guarded eyes, clipped greetings, and quick departures whenever they crossed paths.

The program at St. Raphael ended successfully, the choir receiving applause and admiration. But for Mateo, the music rang hollow. The growing rift with Father Chris, which he could neither explain nor repair, overshadowed the joy of service.

As the school year drew to a close, Father Chris once again invited Mateo to continue assisting at St. Raphael in the coming year. But this time, Mateo hesitated. The memory of the girl's tears, the sight of suspicion in Father Chris' eyes, the heavy burden of secrets not his to keep—all of it weighed too heavily.

"Thank you, Father," Mateo said quietly, "but I think I must focus on my studies here in the seminary."

Father Chris studied him for a moment, his expression unreadable. Then he simply nodded. "As you wish."

Mateo walked away with a heavy heart. He wondered if he had just lost another ally, another friend, to the endless shadows that seemed to follow him in every corner of his priestly pursuit.

Will it always be like this, Lord? he prayed silently. *One step forward, two steps back? Will I ever find peace within Your house?*

The echo of his question lingered unanswered, like the fading notes of a song that refused to resolve.

CHAPTER II

Whispers in the Halls

The year moved on with its rhythm of studies, prayers, and pastoral duties. On the surface, Mateo's life seemed orderly: he attended lectures, delivered polished reports, led choir practices when asked, and even assisted Father Rector in organizational matters. He had earned the respect of many for his discipline and talent.

Yet, under the smooth veneer, something else was stirring—an unease Mateo could neither name nor shake.

It began with small things.

A few seminarians stopped greeting him in the hallways. A conversation would suddenly end when he entered a room. A rumor would pass by his ear,

faint but unmistakable—about his supposed ambition, about his closeness to certain priests, about
things he had never said or done.

At first, Mateo brushed these aside. Every seminary
had its gossip; he was not naïve. But the whispers
grew more pointed. Some suggested that the formators favored him excessively. Others murmured
that his "gifts" made him arrogant, that he thought
himself better than his classmates.

Is this jealousy, Lord? Or is it something more?

The distance with Father Chris only deepened the
sense of isolation. Once, they had shared light meals
after practices, laughter over shared frustrations, and
even a bond of mutual respect. Now their exchanges
were brief and transactional. Mateo felt scrutinized
in his presence, with every word potentially miscon-
strued and every gesture questionable.

He longed to clear the air, to explain what had
really transpired that day at St. Raphael. But how
could he, without dragging the girl's pain further
into the open? No—silence was still the only path he
could take, even if it cost him friendship.

Father Prefect, meanwhile, still sought Mateo's
help occasionally in his garden. Trimming bonsai, arranging potted orchids, or hauling water jugs
across the courtyard offered Mateo some relief—a
reminder that his hands could create beauty, not

just carry burdens. Father Prefect rarely spoke much beyond his plants and the discipline of his fitness routine, but in his quiet presence, Mateo sometimes felt seen, if not fully understood.

But even there, in the stillness of the garden, Mateo caught glimpses of seminarians watching him from the balconies above, whispering as they leaned against the railings. He told himself it was his imagination, but the unease lingered.

The academic load intensified as the second semester began. Mateo thrived in it—his papers were praised, his presentations sharp, and his theology professors impressed by the clarity of his arguments. Yet even here, his excellence became a double-edged sword.

A fellow seminarian once muttered under his breath as they left class, "Of course he gets praised again. Always Mateo."

The sting of resentment hung heavier than the words themselves.

By the time Lent arrived, Mateo could feel the walls closing in. The conspiracies were not yet visible, but the pattern was unmistakable: praise from formators, suspicion from peers, trust in his work, and isolation in his friendships.

He carried it in silence, lifting his prayers each night in his small cell:

Lord, if this is Your way of shaping me, let me endure. But if this is the path to my breaking, then grant me strength to face it without bitterness.

The whispers did not stop. In fact, they began to gather like shadows, unseen but ever-present, biding their time.

Mateo did not yet know it, but the conspiracy against him had already taken root.

CHAPTER 12
The Net Tightens

At first, Mateo thought the shift to Theology would distance him from the shadows of his Philosophy years. A new building, a new rhythm of studies, and even a new circle of peers should have meant a fresh start. He was, after all, the elected president of the theology student body—a role that demanded dignity, leadership, and strength of character.

But the past has a way of reaching forward.

One of those shadows had a name: Rico.

Both Mateo and Rico hailed from the northern part of San Agustin, though Rico was several years older than Mateo. In Philosophy, their paths had crossed only briefly, but long enough for Mateo to remember that Rico always seemed drawn to whispered corners, to secret allegiances. Mateo later discovered why. Rico had been entangled with Miss Lolita, whose influence lingered like a ghost in the corridors of San Agustin and beyond. It was Rico who had carried out her cruel plan to send the fraudulent telegram to the monastery, dragging Mateo home under false grief.

Rico had never been confronted. Mateo had chosen silence and focus over vengeance. But Rico had not forgotten, nor had Miss Lolita released her hold.

Now, under her quiet manipulation, Rico prepared to strike again.

The scheme was simple, yet devastating. Where before the lie had aimed to pull Mateo away from the monastery, this one sought to corrode his reputation from within. The rumor began to circulate: Mateo, despite his humble appearance, was secretly materialistic. He cared too much for recognition, too much for influence, and too much for the admiration that came with his musical fame. Such a man, Rico suggested, was unfit for priesthood.

In casual conversations in the refectory, Rico would drop remarks with careful nonchalance.

"Did you see the way Mateo accepted that award? He looked so proud of himself. Almost... too proud."

Or in the garden:

"Of course he plays the organ so well. But sometimes I wonder—does he do it for God, or for the applause afterward?"

Each comment was small and insignificant on its own. But repeated, whispered, and carried by the hungry ears of seminarians, they began to take root.

What made the rumor dangerous was not just Rico's persistence—it was his proximity to Fr. Alvarez. Even though he was stationed in the Philosophy department, Fr. Alvarez's voice still carried weight. He was, after all, Dean of Studies there and respected across the seminary complex.

Rico knew this was the case And so he sought opportunities to be near him—carrying books to his office, engaging him in "casual" conversation after lectures, always finding ways to seed doubt about Mateo.

"Father," Rico began one afternoon, "I don't mean to judge. But sometimes I wonder if Mateo's heart is truly in the right place. He speaks so beautifully, and he plays so well, but... sometimes I feel he is too attached to how people see him. Too concerned with his image."

Fr. Alvarez listened, silent, letting the words drip like poison. He gave no answer, but Rico noticed the faint narrowing of his eyes. It was enough.

Meanwhile, Mateo remained unaware of the full extent of the scheme. He only felt its shadows—the strange distance in some classmates' eyes, the sudden cooling of what once were easy friendships. When he entered the chapel, conversations seemed to pause. When he spoke at student assemblies, he noticed sidelong glances, as if every word he uttered was being weighed for pride.

At night, under the dim glow of the sanctuary lamp, he prayed:

Lord, why does suspicion follow me everywhere? Have I not sought to serve You with all I am? If I falter, let it be before You alone, not in the mouths of others.

But prayer did not still the unease in his chest.

For while Mateo sought truth and light, others—bound by jealousy, manipulation, and old grudges—were weaving a different story about him, one thread at a time.

And in the Philosophy building, with Rico feeding him quiet suggestions, Fr. Alvarez began to believe it.

CHAPTER 13

The Song and the Snare

Despite being a freshman, Mateo quickly immersed himself in the center of theology's unique pulse and ambitions. Some viewed his election as president of the theology department as remarkable, while others viewed it with suspicion. But to Mateo, it was simply another responsibility, another way of offering himself to service.

If only he had known how others saw it differently.

The whispers seeded by Rico had not died down; in fact, they had begun to grow legs of their own. To some seminarians, Mateo was not merely talented—he was ambitious. To others, he was not merely eloquent—he was proud. Even his music, which once drew admiration, was now quietly spoken of as a tool of vanity.

And always, behind these shadows, there was Rico. He knew the power of Mateo's music, how it stirred hearts and captured attention. And under Miss Lolita's unseen hand, he whispered these doubts with subtle consistency in the ear of Fr. Alvarez.

"Father," he had said one afternoon, pretending to wrestle with his conscience, "sometimes I fear that Mateo is too dependent on his music. It wins him praise everywhere. What if, one day, it becomes more important to him than the priesthood?"

Fr. Alvarez, seated at his Philosophy department desk, folded his hands and remained silent. But his silence was not passive. He was weighing, measuring, and slowly forming a plan.

That plan found its opportunity not within the seminary walls, but outside—back in San Agustin.

For the first time in its history, the city was organizing a songwriting competition, an ambitious project meant to showcase local talent and strengthen cultural pride. Posters and announcements filled the town plazas, inviting composers from the city and surrounding provinces to submit original works. The promise of recognition was immense: the 12 best entries would be chosen to compete in a grand finals concert the following year.

When Mateo saw the announcement, something stirred deep within him. His whole life, music had been a prayer, a channel through which he poured both joy and pain. But now, for the first time, he felt an impulse to offer his music not just within church walls, but to the wider world. It was not pride—it was longing, perhaps even calling. If his music could touch hearts beyond the cloister, perhaps it was another way of serving.

After weeks of prayer and nights at the piano, Mateo composed his entry. The melody was simple yet profound, rising with hope, bending with sorrow, and closing with a quiet strength that reflected his own journey. With trembling hands, he sent it to the competition committee in San Agustin.

What he did not know was that Fr. Alvarez had been appointed chairman of the screening committee.

When the entries came in, the committee gathered in a hall filled with sheet music, tapes, and hopeful names. Some pieces were raw and unpolished; others sparkled with craftsmanship. But when Mateo's entry was played, even the most seasoned musicians paused.

The song rose like incense—haunting, tender, luminous. One of the judges leaned back, eyes closed, and whispered, "This one has something."

Even Fr. Alvarez, in that moment, could not deny its beauty. He felt the pull of its sincerity, the power of its melody. But he also felt something else: the growing unease of watching Mateo's light expand.

He knew instantly that this could be his moment—not to nurture Mateo's gift, but to bend it into the very proof of his suspicion.

And so, Mateo's name was chosen among the 12 finalists.

When the news reached the seminary, Mateo was overwhelmed. To his peers, he laughed shyly and brushed it off, but inside, a quiet joy filled him. He saw it not as a step toward glory but as a chance to honor God in a new way. He prayed:

If this song touches even one heart, Lord, let it be for You, not for me.

Yet outside his prayer, others muttered.

"Of course he got in. Mateo always has to be at the center."

"First president, now a finalist? What's next? A concert tour?"

"He's chasing fame, not holiness."

Each word was like smoke, drifting unseen into the air until it hung over Mateo without his knowledge.

The rules of the competition required that each composer find an interpreter—a singer who would bring the song to life in the grand finals. For Mateo, this became a daunting task. He had written from his soul, but he was no soloist. His voice was for prayer, not the stage. He needed someone who could carry his song with clarity and depth.

He began searching, asking quietly among friends, and contacting acquaintances in San Agustin who might know aspiring singers. He thought little of it, believing it a practical step. However, Fr. Alvarez believed that this was the point at which the trap would begin.

For in choosing an interpreter, Mateo would have to step further outside the seminary walls—into friendships, collaborations, and even public exposure. And every step would be watched, judged, and twisted.

Already, Alvarez was envisioning the narrative he would encourage:

Mateo, the seminarian, was too consumed by his music.

Mateo, who sought applause instead of silence.

Mateo, who looked less like a priest and more like an artist chasing fame.

And so the snare was set.

What Mateo believed to be a blessing—the chance to share his song—would soon become the very stage where envy and manipulation converged against him.

For in the grand finals of San Agustin's first song-writing competition, the applause he sought to give back to God would be used to cast doubt upon the purity of his vocation.

Silently watching from his seat of authority, Fr. Alvarez was already preparing to turn that applause into condemnation.

CHAPTER 14

This Is Not Your Night

The weeks leading up to the grand finals of the San Agustin Songwriting Competition were restless for Mateo.

At first, he had been confident that finding a singer would not be difficult. San Agustin was alive with talent—choirs, soloists, and troubadours who lent their voices at fiestas and civic programs. Mateo approached a few acquaintances, asked friends, and even wrote letters to singers he thought might capture the spirit of his composition.

But one by one, the doors closed. Some had prior commitments. Others expressed hesitation when they learned that the composer was a seminarian—*What if the Church disapproved?* Some simply ignored him.

As the deadline for finalizing interpreters approached, Mateo felt a weight pressing on him. His song had been chosen, but without a voice to deliver it, all his work would end in silence.

After several sleepless nights, he came to a decision: *If no one will sing it, I will sing it myself.*

It was not an easy choice. Mateo had never considered himself a performer. His voice was serviceable in choirs, strong in rehearsals, and prayerful in chapel hymns. But the stage? The lights? The scrutiny of an audience? He had no experience there. Yet he believed in the message of his song, and that belief was enough to steady him.

Determined not to falter, Mateo sought some of the best arrangers in San Agustin—musicians who had worked with local bands, church choirs, and festival productions. Humbly, he presented his composition to them. To his relief, they recognized the beauty in it, and together they crafted an arrangement that brought out its quiet strength.

The rehearsals were grueling. Each week, Mateo would slip away from the seminary, balancing his presidential duties, studies, and practices. He poured himself into every note, adjusting his phrasing, learning how to project, and training his breath.

The arrangers encouraged him, saying, "You can do this. Your song will carry you."

Despite his nerves, Mateo began to feel a quiet anticipation. He prayed constantly, not for victory, but for grace to represent himself and his vocation well. Still, deep within, a hope flickered: perhaps, by God's will, he might even place in the top three.

The grand finals night arrived. The city auditorium was filled to the brim—families, students, civic leaders, and music lovers. Colorful banners draped the hall; the air buzzed with excitement. Each of the 12 finalists would present their entry, backed by professional musicians.

Backstage, Mateo adjusted his borrowed costume, his heart pounding. He glanced at the program booklet, and for the first time, the **list of judges** was announced.

His breath caught.
The Chairman of the Board of Judges: Rev. Fr. Vicente Alvarez.

Mateo's stomach twisted. He had not known until this very moment. The man who had once trained him, then turned against him—the man whose sarcasm still echoed in his memory—was now the one who held sway over the outcome of his song.

He closed his eyes, whispered a prayer, and resolved not to let fear overcome him.

When his turn came, Mateo walked onstage, the lights blinding, the audience hushed. He took a breath, signaled to the band, and began.

The song rose gently, each line shaped by the months of labor, each note carrying the weight of his journey. He sang not as a performer but as one offering a prayer. And for a few moments, it felt as if the whole hall leaned in, listening not to a seminarian or a contestant, but to a soul opening itself in music.

Applause followed, warm and generous. Mateo bowed, heart still racing, and left the stage with trembling hands.

The competition continued, each entry met with cheers and applause. When the final performance was over, the judges withdrew to deliberate. Whispers spread backstage, singers paced, and composers clutched one another's arms in nervous hope.

Finally, the results were announced. Third place. Second place. First place.

None were Mateo.

A brief flicker of disappointment burned in his chest, but he forced a smile, clapped for the winners, and whispered to himself, *"Thy will be done."*

Later, as the hall emptied and he returned backstage to change out of his costume, he felt a presence behind him.

A breath.

A whisper.

"This is not your night, Mateo."

The voice was low and deliberate.

Mateo froze, then turned his head slightly. There was Fr. Alvarez, standing just behind him, a thin smile curling at his lips. His eyes gleamed not with kindness, but with something sharper—triumph cloaked in mockery.

For a moment, neither spoke. Then Alvarez stepped away, disappearing into the shadows of the corridor, leaving Mateo with only the echo of his words.

Mateo sat down, staring at the floor. A knot tightened in his chest. Yet even in the sting of defeat and humiliation, he whispered a prayer into the silence:

Lord, if this is not my night, then teach me to wait for Yours.

CHAPTER 15

Whispers of Vanity

When Mateo returned to the theology seminary after the songwriting competition, he carried himself with quiet dignity. He did not bring up the event unless someone asked. A few seminarians congratulated him for having been a finalist at all—"Twelve songs chosen out of hundreds! That's no small feat." He accepted their words with humility, smiling politely, yet he said little. Inside, he still carried the sting of disappointment and that lingering whisper from backstage: *This is not your night, Mateo.*

But the walls of a seminary had ears sharper than most places. What one person muttered could echo down corridors and slip into refectories. It wasn't long before comments began to surface.

At first, they were innocent: *"I heard Mateo sang at the city competition."*
Then speculative: *"Do you think it's proper for a seminarian to be competing like that?"*
And soon accusatory: *"He is chasing fame. Where is the humility of a priest?"*

Behind these whispers was a careful hand, steady and deliberate. Fr. Alvarez.

Although he was still based in the Philosophy Department, his influence easily extended into Theology. Professors met, priests conversed, and seminarians mingled across departments. It took only a word, a suggestion over coffee, or a raised brow during recreation to plant the seed that Mateo was letting his gift for music become a ladder to worldly ambition.

Rico, still loyal to Miss Lolita and all too willing to wound Mateo further, became the perfect echo. He was seen repeating the same phrases Alvarez had murmured: *"Mateo wants applause more than prayer. He seeks the stage more than the altar."*

Mateo, meanwhile, immersed himself in his responsibilities as student body president. He managed meetings, organized community service projects, balanced academics, and attended choir rehearsals.

Outwardly, he seemed composed. But inside, the rumors scraped at him.

In one faculty meeting, a priest casually remarked, "It's a pity, Mateo. You must be careful not to lose sight of your vocation with all this music."

The words struck deep. Mateo had never thought of his song as vanity—it had been an offering, his way of contributing beauty to the world. But now, each compliment he received was laced with suspicion, each opportunity shadowed by doubt.

One evening, Mateo sat in his room with his guitar across his lap, the strings silent beneath his fingers, and prayed aloud:

"Lord, You gave me this gift. Was it wrong to use it? Did I stray from Your path? If so, forgive me. But if not, strengthen me against these whispers. Let me not be swayed by malice or envy."

He closed his eyes, and in that silence, a memory surfaced—the words of his Abbot long ago, on the island of the Trappists: *Divine Providence works even through confusion. Trust, and you will see.*

Days turned into weeks. The sting of the competition faded, but the shadow of Alvarez's scheme remained. Mateo noticed how some seminarians grew distant, how others looked at him with questions in their eyes. But he responded only with kindness, humility, and diligence.

If Alvarez intended to discredit him, Mateo resolved that his life itself—his work, his service, his discipline—would be his defense.

And so he pressed on.

But he knew, deep in his heart, this was not the last move Alvarez would make.

CHAPTER 16

Shadows Before the Pope

The whole city of San Agustin was alive with anticipation. It was February 1981—news spread like wildfire: **Pope John Paul II was coming.** For weeks, preparations filled the air—banners strung across streets, makeshift stages erected, and choirs rehearsing in every corner of the diocese. For the seminarians, this was more than just a historic visit; it was a once-in-a-lifetime honor.

The diocesan seminary, with its three departments—high school, philosophy, and theology—was to provide the core of the great choir for the papal Mass at the old San Agustin airport. The responsibility fell, naturally, under the meticulous eye of Fr.

Alvarez, who, as head of the liturgical committee, dictated the rehearsals down to the smallest detail.

For Mateo, standing among his fellow theology seminarians, the rehearsals were exhausting but exhilarating. Each day, as the voices swelled in harmony, he felt a swell of pride. To sing for the Pope was not just a privilege—it was a sacred offering.

A few days before the Pontiff's arrival, a general rehearsal was held at the grand open stage prepared on the tarmac of the old airport. The sun was merciless that morning, but the voices of hundreds of seminarians soared. "Again," Fr. Alvarez commanded, waving his hand as the final chord faded. Sweat dripped down faces, feet ached, but no one dared complain.

Finally, as dusk crept over the horizon, the rehearsal ended. Groups of seminarians began their long walk back to their respective buildings. Laughter, chatter, and the shuffle of sandals on the pavement filled the streets.

Mateo walked with a cluster of theology classmates, their black cassocks swaying slightly in the evening breeze. His back was damp with sweat, but his heart was light. "Imagine," one of the seminarians said, "our voices reaching the ears of the Holy Father."

But then, without warning, the night turned violent.

A sudden, crushing blow struck Mateo across the back and head. He stumbled forward, then collapsed into the middle of the road, dazed. A heavy object—a blunt force—had been hurled or swung at him. The world blurred, sounds muffled, and darkness threatened to pull him under.

"Help..." his voice cracked, barely a whisper. He tried to lift himself, his arms trembling. But instead of help, he heard the sharp sound of sandals slapping the pavement—the hurried retreat of his companions. Fear scattered them.

"Please..." he gasped again, though his vision dimmed.

Alone now, Mateo clawed at the ground, dragging himself toward the edge of the road. Each movement burned through his back, each breath a struggle. The smell of dust filled his nostrils. Somehow, inch by inch, he made it to the seminary gate, where the world tilted and he nearly collapsed again.

By what he would later call Providence, a seminarian assigned as driver for the theology department's vehicle came rushing from the gatehouse. He spotted Mateo's crumpled form and cried out. "Mateo! What happened?"

Without waiting for an answer, he lifted Mateo into the vehicle and sped toward the nearest hospital. Mateo's eyes fluttered open and shut, pain pressing him deeper into unconsciousness. The sound of the engine roared in his ears. He thought about the upcoming visit of the Pope. He thought of the choir. He thought of the whisper he had prayed so many times before: *Lord, grant me strength.*

For the next several days, Mateo lay in a white hospital bed, bandages wrapped around his head, his back sore and bruised. Doctors reassured him that his injuries were not permanent, but they stressed the importance of rest.

But when the day of the papal Mass finally came—the voices rising in glorious unison before Pope John Paul II, the faithful filling the airport field—Mateo was not there. He listened from afar, through a small radio at the hospital, his eyes moist as the hymns floated across the airwaves.

He did not understand why it happened. Why had he been attacked? Why had the others fled, leaving him alone? Who had wanted to harm him so deliberately?

The questions remained unanswered. All he knew was that he had been struck down on the eve of one of the greatest moments of his life in the seminary.

And somewhere deep inside him, a quiet unease began to grow.

CHAPTER 17

Whispers in the Dark

The attack left scars that no bandage could hide. Mateo returned from the hospital outwardly healed, his body steady again, but deep inside him something had shifted. He was no longer the same serene and trusting seminarian who once walked the seminary corridors in simple confidence.

Now, there was a weight inside him—a flame of anger that refused to be extinguished. He wanted to know who had done this to him. He wanted to stare into their eyes, to ask why, and perhaps even to make them pay.

But all he had was one faint memory: as the blow struck him, a voice had hissed near his ear—

"This is the target, fellows."

The words haunted him.

Mateo began his own quiet, covert investigation. He was careful, speaking to no one in the seminary. During his recovery days, he reached out to his old contact—the private investigator who had once traced the fraudulent telegram that nearly destroyed him at the Trappist Monastery. The man listened carefully to Mateo's account, then nodded with grim certainty.

"Leave it to me. I'll find them. I'll find out who ordered this."

Mateo agreed, his heart restless but resigned.

For weeks, the investigator followed leads through the back alleys of San Agustin. And slowly, the truth began to take shape: five street thugs. Paid. Ready. They were not random criminals. They were assigned.

The investigator gave Mateo their names, their descriptions, and their hideouts. Mateo listened in silence, his fists tightening under the table. He wanted to act, to confront them, but the investigator raised a hand.

"Not yet. I'll dig deeper. You need to focus on your studies. You should also prioritize your safety. Let me uncover who's pulling the strings."

Mateo nodded reluctantly. He knew he had to wait, though the fire in his chest burned hotter with every passing day.

When he returned to the seminary after his discharge, life appeared normal on the surface. He rejoined classes, resumed his responsibilities, and continued the duties of being student-body president. But inside, he was always watchful. Always listening.

Then, unexpectedly, a new path opened before him.

One afternoon, as Mateo rested by the seminary courtyard, a visiting priest approached him. He was middle-aged, with a gentle smile and a voice that carried the cadence of the northern towns.

"I am Fr. Rowel, from Santa Teresa Parish," he introduced himself. "I've spoken to your Rector. He agreed to lend you to us for a special project."

Mateo raised an eyebrow, unsure what the statement meant.

"We are preparing for a golden wedding anniversary—a generous benefactor who helped rebuild our parish church. We want the celebration to be filled with music worthy of the occasion. The choir is… let's just say, in need of guidance." He chuckled softly. "Would you be willing to help?"

The request startled Mateo, yet warmed him. He had barely recovered from the shadows of his attack, and now he was being invited again to use his gifts for something good.

"Of course, Father," Mateo answered with a polite bow. "If the Rector has already given his permission, I will gladly serve."

The arrangement was soon set. Every Saturday morning, Mateo would be driven from the seminary to Santa Teresa Parish. He would spend several hours with the parish choir—training them in vocal discipline, polishing harmonies, and teaching them hymns for the celebration. By late afternoon, he would return to the seminary in time for **Vespers.**

The first Saturday he arrived at Santa Teresa, the choir greeted him with nervous smiles. They were ordinary parishioners—shopkeepers, students, mothers, workers—all bound by their love of singing, though their voices were rough and untrained. Mateo listened patiently to their first attempt at a hymn and then smiled, despite their hesitant notes.

"We'll get there," he reassured them. "Music is not just about sound—it's about heart. And if you sing from here"—he placed a hand on his chest—"it will reach the heavens."

They leaned in, eager, and under his guidance, the music began to take shape.

In the evenings, back at the seminary, Mateo often thought of the double life he was now living. By day, the diligent theology student. By night, the silent investigator of his own tragedy. And on Saturdays, the parish choir director.

The threads of his life tangled, pulling him in different directions, yet in each one, he felt God's hand, mysterious and unrelenting.

Still, when he lay on his narrow bed at night, the words would echo again in his mind:

"This is the target, fellows."

And he would tighten his fists under the blanket, vowing that one day, he would learn who had spoken them.

CHAPTER 18

The Don on the Hill

Santa Teresa Parish had quickly become a second home for Mateo. Every Saturday, he arrived with a small satchel of scores and a stack of fresh lyrics, ready to shape the parish choir into something resembling harmony. What had once been a patchwork of timid voices was now a body of singers who carried themselves with growing confidence. Their blend was far from perfect, but Mateo could already hear the faint outlines of a choir that could move hearts.

Children sang beside their grandparents. Farmers' wives sang with schoolteachers. Even the town tailor joined in, his gravelly bass adding depth to the hymns. For Mateo, it was not just music—it was a communion of lives woven together by voices.

That Saturday, midway through rehearsal, Fr. Rowel paused, raised his hand, and beckoned someone forward.

"Choir, I'd like to introduce a very important guest," he said.

From the back, a man stepped forward with measured steps. He was tall, broad-shouldered, and dressed in a crisp barong that shimmered faintly under the church's dim lights. His presence drew silence the way gravity pulls at the tide. Even before his name was spoken, the choir members bowed their heads slightly out of habit, as if in recognition of power.

"This is Don Alberto," Fr. Rowel announced with a smile. "The benefactor of our parish. A man whose generosity made this church what it is today."

Mateo rose quickly and bowed his head. "It's an honor to meet you, Don Alberto."

The Don's handshake was strong, firm enough to remind Mateo of a vise grip. His eyes, sharp and calculating, searched Mateo's face. After a moment, he spoke.

"I've heard much about you, young man. You lead well. They say you were attacked some weeks ago, yet here you are—alive, teaching, singing. That kind of resilience earns respect."

Mateo said nothing at first, startled by how swiftly the Don had shifted from formality to familiarity. "God has been merciful," he finally replied.

The Don gave a slight nod, then turned to the choir. "I have a special request. My grandchildren must join this choir. They are lively, perhaps too lively, but I want them to sing on the day of my golden wedding anniversary. Teach them as you would the others."

Mateo smiled. "It would be my joy to do so."

The choir clapped politely. The Don placed a hand on Mateo's shoulder before leaving. That simple gesture felt less like affection and more like a mark of ownership.

The following weeks brought the Don's grandchildren into the fold—four bright-eyed children whose laughter filled the parish hall. They were playful, often forgetting their lines in favor of chasing each other around the pews, but Mateo found himself smiling despite the extra work.

Little by little, the children took their places in the choir. Their pure, high voices added a new lightness to the hymns. Parishioners who dropped in on rehearsals often left smiling, whispering that the golden wedding Mass would be unlike anything the parish had ever seen.

For Mateo, these afternoons brought a rare sense of peace. Here, among children and music, the shadows of the seminary politics seemed far away.

But one late afternoon, after rehearsal, peace gave way to something else.

"Mateo," Fr. Rowel said as he wiped his brow, "Don Alberto would like to see you at his home. He insists."

Mateo hesitated. "His home?"

"Yes, up the hill. He said it's important."

The drive was short but steep. The road wound upward, bordered by tall acacia trees. When the car crested the final turn, Mateo saw it: a grand mansion perched high above the town, its white walls gleaming in the last rays of sunset. From this vantage point, Santa Teresa lay quiet and small, as though the entire town were at Don Alberto's feet.

Inside, the mansion smelled faintly of polished wood and cigar smoke. The study they entered was lined with shelves of leather-bound books, each spine perfectly aligned. Framed photographs covered the walls: Don Alberto shaking hands with generals, bishops, and even the President himself.

The Don waved Mateo to a chair. "Sit, young man. Have some juice."

Mateo accepted the glass, his hands slightly damp with nervousness.

The Don leaned forward. His voice, though calm, carried an edge.

"I heard what happened to you. The attack. Five men, was it? Street rats."

Mateo froze. He had not spoken of the details, not even to most seminarians. His private investigator friend was the only one who knew more than fragments.

"Yes, Don," Mateo said cautiously. "But I am better now. I survived."

Don Alberto's eyes narrowed. "Surviving is not enough. You must make sure they never try again."

He opened a drawer and pulled out a small handgun. Its cold gleam seemed to drain the air from the room.

"This," the Don said, sliding it across the desk, "is for your protection. I cannot allow a guest of my parish—or a servant of God—to be left defenseless."

Mateo's breath caught. He stared at the weapon as though it were a serpent coiled to strike.

"I… I cannot, Don Alberto," he said softly. "I am a seminarian. My calling is to preach peace, not carry arms."

The Don chuckled darkly. "And yet, peace alone does not stop a knife in the dark. I will not have your blood on my conscience. Take it."

He pushed it closer. The wood of the desk scraped faintly under the weight.

Mateo pulled back, his palms sweating. "Don, please. My trust is in God. I cannot."

The Don's smile faded, replaced by a stern, almost paternal look. "You are brave—but also naïve. Very well. Keep your prayers. I will take care of those who touched you. You need not lift a finger."

The words chilled Mateo more than the sight of the gun. He bowed his head, murmured a thank you, and rose quickly.

As he left the grand house and descended the hill, the lights of Santa Teresa twinkled below. The evening air was cool, but inside, Mateo's heart burned with unease.

Yes, the choir thrived. Yes, Don Alberto's grandchildren brought laughter to his Saturdays. But now, in the shadows of power, Mateo felt the tug of something dangerous—something that threatened to pull him into a world far darker than he had ever known.

For the first time, he wondered: Was his service at Santa Teresa merely about music? Or had God led him here to test the boundaries of his faith against temptation, power, and violence?

CHAPTER 19

Shadows of Protection

The Saturdays at Santa Teresa Parish carried with them an odd duality. Outwardly, life had never looked brighter. The choir grew strong under Mateo's direction, the voices of Don Alberto's grandchildren ringing like silver bells across the nave. Parishioners spoke of the upcoming golden wedding with excitement, whispering that even the President himself would soon walk through their church doors.

But beneath that glow, Mateo's spirit trembled. Every time he saw Don Alberto sitting at the back of the church, arms folded across his chest as he watched the rehearsal, Mateo felt as though the man were weighing him, measuring whether he would bend—or break.

The memory of the gun still haunted him. He could still feel its cold presence on the Don's desk, gleaming under the study lamp, accompanied by words spoken not as a suggestion but as a law. *I will take care of those who touched you.*

It might have been bravado, Mateo thought. Perhaps an empty show of power. Yet part of him knew that men like Don Alberto did not speak idly.

That certainty came crashing down a few weeks later.

The knock at the seminary gate came just after dinner. The porter called for Mateo, and there, waiting with a quiet air of secrecy, was his private investigator friend. The man's eyes darted left and right, making sure no one was listening.

"We need to talk," he whispered.

They walked together to the darkened edge of the garden, away from the glow of the chapel lamps. The investigator took a deep breath.

"Mateo… you won't believe what I found. Or rather, what I've failed to find."

"What do you mean?" Mateo asked, anxiety tightening his chest.

"Your attackers. The five men. They're gone."

Mateo blinked. "Gone?"

"One by one," the man continued, his voice low, "they've disappeared. Two were found dead—supposedly accidents. One fell off a scaffolding; the other was stabbed in a drunken brawl. But listen to this: two more boarded a bus trying to get out of San Agustin. The bus never reached its destination. It went off a cliff. Everyone on board perished."

Mateo's stomach turned. "And the fifth?"

"He was arrested last week for robbery. Picked up by the police. But before his trial even began, he was killed inside the jail. Word is he got into a fight with another inmate. Very convenient."

The investigator paused, his gaze sharp. "That doesn't happen by chance, Mateo. This was no string of coincidences. Someone... removed them. One by one."

Mateo's knees weakened. He reached for the low garden wall and steadied himself. "But... who would—"

The investigator cut in. "That's what I'm still working on. I don't have the smoking gun yet. But someone powerful wanted those men silenced. Someone who wanted to protect you—or protect themselves. Mateo..." He hesitated, then asked quietly, "You've had contact with Don Alberto, haven't you?"

Mateo swallowed hard. He remembered the Don's hand sliding the pistol across the desk. The cold certainty in his voice. *I will take care of those who touched you.*

His silence was answer enough.

The investigator leaned closer. "Be careful with that man. He's not the kind you can simply thank and walk away from. His help always comes with a price."

Mateo nodded, though his throat felt tight. When the investigator left, disappearing into the night, Mateo remained standing under the trees, his mind churning.

That night, he could not sleep. He lay on his narrow seminary bed, staring at the ceiling. The faces of the five attackers flashed before him—not out of pity, but as a grim reminder. Whoever they were, whatever they had done, they had been men of flesh and blood. Now, they were nothing but ashes and memories.

And why? Because someone had decided their lives were no longer convenient.

Was Don Alberto truly his protector? Or had the Don simply used him as an excuse to demonstrate his reach, to remind him that nothing in Santa Teresa—or perhaps even in San Agustin—happened without his hand?

Mateo pressed his palms together and prayed. But even prayer that night felt heavy, as though God's silence weighed down upon him.

In his heart, one question grew louder with every passing hour:

How can I serve God in a world where protection comes in blood and fear?

Chapter 20

The Shadow of Power

The days at Santa Teresa Parish grew tense as the golden wedding drew near. What began as a joyful project of teaching hymns to children and elderly alike now carried an air of restrained fear. The parish choir rehearsed with more urgency, each singer aware that this would not be just another church celebration. This was history unfolding in their midst.

One Saturday afternoon, as Mateo walked up the narrow road that wound toward Don Alberto's house on the hill, he stopped short. The air was thick with the low growl of military engines. A convoy of olive-green trucks rumbled past him, their wheels grinding the dust into choking clouds.

Soldiers in full combat gear, rifles slung across their chests, stared coldly at every passerby.

An old woman carrying vegetables quickly stepped off the road, bowing her head as though the mere sight of the soldiers demanded submission. Children who usually played by the roadside scattered into doorways, their laughter silenced. Mateo felt his pulse quicken. This was no ordinary security measure. This was an occupation.

By the time he reached the plaza in front of the parish church, the entire town square had been transformed. Camouflaged soldiers stood at every corner, their eyes sharp, their movements precise. A machine gun nest had been set up near the entrance of the municipal hall. Even the bell tower of Santa Teresa Parish bore the silhouette of a sniper crouching in the shadows.

Mateo whispered to himself, "So this is what it takes for the First Couple to come here."

Inside the parish hall, the choir was waiting, trying to rehearse as if nothing had changed. Yet every note of their hymn seemed to tremble against the heavy silence of boots and rifles outside. Mateo lifted his hands, guiding them through the piece, but he could feel their fear—the children glancing at the windows, the adults forcing their voices through dry throats.

At the break, Fr. Rowel approached him quietly. "Mateo, this is what power looks like. When Don Alberto hosts, the entire nation bows."

Mateo forced a smile, but his heart ached. Was this still a celebration of love, a golden wedding in the eyes of God? Or had it become a demonstration of political theater, wrapped in hymns and candles?

Later that afternoon, Mateo accompanied Fr. Rowel to Don Alberto's mansion. The road leading up the hill was lined with checkpoints. Military men inspected every vehicle, their fingers never straying far from their triggers. A helicopter buzzed overhead, circling the estate before vanishing toward the horizon.

Inside the mansion, the atmosphere was starkly different. Crystal chandeliers glowed, polished floors reflected the sunlight, and laughter echoed in the hallways. Don Alberto greeted Mateo with his usual commanding warmth, his arm draped casually over the shoulder of one of his grandsons.

"My boy," the Don said, "you see how my friends prepare for me? Even Malacañang trusts Santa Teresa to be safe."

Mateo nodded politely, though unease coiled in his stomach. He remembered the investigator's report, the silent fates of the five men who had attacked him. He could almost hear the whisper again—*I will take care of those who touched you.*

Don Alberto's words now seemed less like hospitality and more like prophecy.

That night, back in his seminary room, Mateo sat by the window staring at the quiet campus. His ears still rang with the echo of boots on cobblestones, the hum of engines, and the uneasy hymns of the choir.

He pressed his hand over his chest and prayed, *"Lord, let my music honor You, not men." Let my voice carry truth, not fear. Keep me steady when power tempts me, when its shadow falls too close.*

But in the silence that followed, Mateo wondered if the God he sought to serve could still be found in a world so bound by power, fear, and invisible bargains.

Chapter 21
The Golden Wedding

The morning sun broke over Santa Teresa like a curtain rising on a grand theater. From the first rays of dawn, the town no longer felt like itself. Every corner bore the stamp of authority. Camouflaged trucks were parked in rows along the main road. Armed men lined the sidewalks, their eyes sweeping the crowd with mechanical precision. Banners of gold and white fluttered in the wind, announcing a celebration of love, yet the heavy presence of rifles and radios told another story—this was more than a wedding anniversary. This was a stage for power.

By mid-morning, the plaza outside Santa Teresa Parish was packed. Farmers in their cleanest shirts, women in brightly pressed skirts, and children clutching their parents' hands—all pressed together in hushed anticipation. No one dared speak too loudly. The whispers that moved through the crowd were about motorcades, generals, and the First Lady's dress.

Inside the church, Mateo stood before the choir. His cassock clung to him with the weight of sweat and nervousness. He raised his arms and gave them a gentle nod. The children inhaled together, the first notes rising like fragile wings. Their voices floated upward, echoing against the stained-glass windows. It was a sound pure enough to momentarily wash away the tension that gripped the town.

But as the last chord faded, the silence outside cracked into thunder. Sirens wailed. Engines roared. The presidential motorcade had arrived.

Through the church doors, Mateo glimpsed the convoy: sleek black limousines crawling through the crowd, flanked by motorcycles and jeeps bristling with soldiers. A swarm of cameras flashed, reporters jostled, and people stretched their necks just to catch a glimpse.

When the President and his wife stepped out, the air itself seemed to bow. He, in his immaculate barong, raised a hand in controlled confidence. She, radiant in a gown of pearls and ivory, smiled with practiced grace. The crowd erupted into a roar that was equal parts devotion and fear.

Don Alberto stood at the church entrance, waiting like a king welcoming royalty. His white suit glistened in the sun, his gold cane tapping the ground with every step. He bent low to greet the First Couple, kissing the First Lady's hand and shaking the President's firmly. For a moment, the crowd forgot the rifles, forgot the soldiers, and forgot the unease. All eyes were on that union of wealth, faith, and political might.

The mass began.

The bishop presided, his voice solemn as he blessed Don Alberto and his wife. The people's gaze magnified every gesture of the First Couple as they sat in gilded chairs near the altar. Around them, generals, governors, and foreign diplomats filled the pews.

When the offer arrived, Mateo lifted his hand. The choir's entrance was soft, angelic, yet filled with a trembling power. The organ swelled behind them, and the voices of children and youth rose like a river of light, weaving through the incense that curled toward the vaulted ceiling.

Mateo sang with them, his own voice steady but his heart divided. Every note was for God, yet every applause and glance from the crowd seemed directed toward the powerful person seated at the altar. He could feel it—the music being claimed, not as worship, but as a jewel in Don Alberto's crown.

At the communion hymn, Mateo caught sight of the Don's glance. Don Alberto looked at him from across the nave, eyes gleaming with pride, as though he were saying, *"See, my boy? Even your voice serves the empire I have built."*

Outside, a military band burst into brass fanfares as the mass ended. Doves were released, rising against the blue sky. Confetti rained from the balconies. The people erupted in cheers as the First Couple emerged, holding hands with Don Alberto and his wife. It was a spectacle of unity, of wealth and power draped in the garments of faith.

But as Mateo stood in the choir loft, watching the soldiers salute, the cameras flash, and the crowd scream, a shiver passed through him.

He realized that this was not just a golden wedding. It was a coronation.

And somehow, through song, he had been made a part of it.

CHAPTER 22

The Weight of a Song

That night, after the last fireworks had faded and the echoes of applause were only memories carried in the wind, Mateo lay awake in his narrow seminary bed. His cassock hung neatly on the chair beside him, still carrying the faint trace of incense and perfume from the celebration. His hands, folded on his chest, were restless. He could still feel the vibrations of the choir's voices, the organ's swell, and the sound of children lifting their song to heaven.

But the memory was not pure.

Each note, once holy, now seemed tainted—wrapped in the glittering image of the First Couple, of Don Alberto's golden smile, of generals saluting under the altar's shadow. What had begun as worship had become a performance, a gift wrapped and presented not to God, but to power. And Mateo had been the ribbon tied on top.

He replayed it in his mind: the First Lady's smile as the children sang, the President's subtle nod of approval, and Don Alberto's proud glance across the nave. Every gesture carried the weight of possession. They had claimed the music, claimed the voices, and claimed him.

And what gnawed at Mateo's conscience was not just the pageantry—it was the applause.

He remembered how his heart swelled when the people clapped, how his chest warmed with pride when whispers spread in the pews about the young seminarian leading the choir. That dangerous sweetness lingered. For a moment, he had felt important, even indispensable. And that terrified him.

Was this how temptation began—not with sin, but with admiration? Not with rebellion, but with applause?

Turning to his side, Mateo buried his face into the pillow, ashamed of the pride he could not shake. He thought of his vow, his calling, and his dream of serving God in humility. But tonight, in Santa Teresa, it seemed that music had not lifted souls to heaven—it had been dragged down into the machinery of politics and vanity.

Don Alberto's words haunted him most of all: *"Even your music can protect you, Mateo. Even your music can serve."*

But serve whom? God, or men?

The seminary was quiet. Outside, the cicadas sang their endless chorus. Mateo stared into the dark, feeling that the silence between those insect calls was like an unanswered question lodged in his soul.

He prayed, but his words stumbled. He searched for peace, but his conscience kept replaying the sight of soldiers standing guard with rifles during a mass. He wanted to tell himself that he had done nothing wrong—that he had only lifted his voice for God. Yet deep inside, he knew his gift had been used, and perhaps, in some corner of his heart, he had allowed it to be used.

Sleep never came easily that night. When it did, it carried him into dreams where his song was no longer a hymn but a trumpet of power, echoing across a darkened plaza where faceless men in uniforms marched to his music.

And in the dream, Mateo tried to silence them—but his voice only grew louder.

CHAPTER 23

Threads of the Past

The following week, Mateo sat across the polished wooden table in the seminary's small study room, the shutters closed against the afternoon sun. His private investigator, a wiry man with sharp eyes and the air of someone who could blend into shadows, leaned forward with a folder in hand.

"I told you I would find out who ordered it," he said in a low voice, sliding the folder toward Mateo. "And now I can say with certainty—it was not random. It was planned."

Mateo's throat tightened. His hand hovered above the folder but hesitated to touch it. "Planned?" he echoed.

The investigator nodded. "Five men carried out the assault. But the voice you heard—the one who whispered, 'This is the target.'—came from one of Rico's old associates. Rico himself wasn't there, but he arranged it."

The name hit Mateo like a stone. Rico. A familiar figure from his town of San Agustin, once a senior in the Philosophy Department, now a shadow that kept returning in different disguises.

"Why?" Mateo asked, his voice barely above a whisper.

The investigator's gaze sharpened. "Because Rico was working under orders. The woman who pulled the strings is someone you already know. Miss Lolita."

Mateo sat back, stunned. Miss Lolita—the same woman whose schemes had once nearly destroyed him with the fraudulent telegram. The same woman whose charm had twisted seminarians like Rico into pawns. He remembered the rumors, the whispered stories of her influence, her closeness with certain priests.

"Are you certain?" Mateo finally managed.

The investigator tapped the folder. "Inside are names, connections, and the payments made. Rico still has ties to the street gangs in San Agustin. He called in favors. Miss Lolita was the one who wanted you silenced. Perhaps not killed, but humiliated, broken, and weakened. You're rising too quickly, Mateo. Too much recognition, too much influence. Some people fear that."

The words pierced deeper than the physical wounds he still carried. His attack had not been the work of strangers. It was betrayal—rooted in the tangled web of seminary politics, ambition, and jealousy.

When Mateo opened the folder, photographs, notes, and names blurred before his eyes. He saw familiar corners of San Agustin marked with arrows, timelines of movements and payments handed discreetly in dark alleys. And there, in neat handwriting, was the link between Rico and Miss Lolita.

His chest grew heavy. Part of him wanted to storm into Rico's quarters, confront him, and demand answers. Another part wanted to stand before Miss Lolita and shout the truth into her face. Yet, deep down, Mateo knew this was larger than a single confrontation.

This was a war of shadows, where accusations would only tighten the traps set against him.

In the weeks that followed, Mateo noticed Rico's presence more acutely than ever. He was no longer just another seminarian from San Agustin. Rico had wormed his way into the theology circles with an uncanny ability to win the trust of those around him. He lingered at the edges of group conversations, dropping subtle remarks about Mateo's growing reputation.

"Music is beautiful," Rico would say with a faint smile, "but sometimes it makes one forget the humility of silence." Or, "Mateo is so talented, no doubt, but one wonders if he seeks the priesthood… or the spotlight."

These comments were always wrapped in piety, offered like harmless observations. But little by little, they spread through the dormitories, whispered in refectories, and carried into classrooms. A seed of doubt was being planted in the minds of his peers: Was Mateo still the humble seminarian they once admired, or was he becoming a man intoxicated by fame?

Mateo recognized the hand behind the game. Rico was Miss Lolita's pawn, carrying her venom into the very air Mateo breathed. And somewhere behind Rico, Mateo could almost sense the approving shadow of Fr. Alvarez, who had never abandoned his quiet mission of control.

The investigator warned him, "Don't react too soon. They thrive on your anger. Keep silent; let your deeds speak. Truth has its own way of breaking through."

But silence was heavy. Every time Mateo walked past Rico in the hallways and saw the glint of sly confidence in his eyes, he felt a tightening in his chest. He remembered the whisper in the street—*"This is the target, fellows."* He remembered the blood on his shirt, the lonely crawl to the seminary gate. And now, he realized that the same hand was once again working against him, not in the streets this time, but within the hearts of his brothers.

That night, in the quiet of his room, Mateo prayed not for vengeance but for endurance. His words trembled on his lips as he asked God for the grace to rise above the shadows. Yet, even as he prayed, he knew: the war was only beginning.

Chapter 24

An Island's Embrace

The semester had finally ended, and with it came the long-awaited two-week break from seminary life. For most of the seminarians, it was a time to return to their families, revisit hometowns, or simply bask in the familiarity of places that had shaped them before the walls of theology confined their days. For Mateo, however, this break felt different. He needed air—distance not only from the seminary but also from the shadows that had grown around him in recent months.

So, instead of returning to San Agustin, Mateo made a quiet decision: he would spend his break visiting a distant relative on another island. The journey itself was long, a full day's travel by bus and ferry, and he welcomed it. The farther the ferry pulled away from the mainland, the more Mateo felt the weight of recent struggles—rumors, sabotage, the painful attack that had nearly cost him his life—slip, if only slightly, into the sea behind him.

When he arrived, the island greeted him with a slower rhythm of life. Coconut palms bent in the wind, fishermen returned with their catch at dawn, and children laughed barefoot along the sandy roads. His relative, a kindly aunt with a small bamboo house on the edge of the village, welcomed him warmly. "Here, nephew, you will rest," she said, setting a plate of steaming rice and dried fish before him on his first night.

Mateo embraced the quiet. Each morning he would walk the shoreline, letting the salt wind brush his face, and in the afternoons he would sit beneath the shade of an old acacia tree, notebook in hand. Sometimes he jotted fragments of prayers, sometimes lyrics to songs that came to him unbidden. Other times he simply watched the horizon and allowed silence to fill the space where suspicion and fear had lived too long.

But rest was incomplete. At night, when the village hushed into darkness, Mateo would lie awake and replay the strange web of his recent past: Fr. Chris and the broken friendship, the smear campaign by Rico, and the shadow of Miss Lolita's interference. And most haunting of all—the unanswered question of why God seemed to allow such trials to pile one upon another.

Still, the island gave him something the seminary rarely could: perspective. Away from the scrutiny of peers and the ambitions of superiors, he was simply Mateo again—not the seminary president, not the target of rumor or attack, but a young man struggling to find God's peace in the midst of chaos. One evening, as he watched the sun dissolve into the horizon, he whispered a prayer that surprised even himself:

"Lord, if suffering is my path, then teach me how to carry it without bitterness."

In that moment, the sea breeze swept over him gently, almost as if to assure him that, though peace was not yet his, it was not beyond his reach.

By the end of the two weeks, Mateo felt both reluctant and ready. The seminary awaited him with its demands, its politics, and its quiet storms. But somewhere deep inside, the island had given him a small ember of renewal—a reminder that though the battles continued, his heart still longed for service, still longed for God.

With his small bag slung over his shoulder, he boarded the ferry back, the waves carrying him once more toward San Agustin and the uncertain road ahead.

CHAPTER 25

Shadows in the Theater

The ferry pulled into the port of San Agustin just as the late afternoon sun cast a golden shimmer across the water. Mateo stood at the railing, his bag hanging loosely from his shoulder. The days on the island had given him a sense of calm, but he knew the peace was fragile. Ahead lay the seminary with its quiet storms and the lives that had become entangled with his own in ways he had yet to fully untangle.

Before heading back to the seminary, Mateo reached for a familiar thread of comfort: Nick. His loyal friend had always been a steady presence, one of the few who neither used nor suspected him. "I'll be in the city tonight," Mateo told him over the phone. "Want to catch a movie?"

Nick, quick as always, replied, "Of course. I'll bring along a friend."

Mateo thought nothing of it, imagining another seminarian or a childhood acquaintance. Only when the three met outside the theater did he realize Nick had brought a young woman. Her name was Carolina—slender, soft-spoken, with eyes that darted shyly between Mateo and Nick. She extended her hand politely, and Mateo, a little taken aback but always courteous, returned the gesture.

The three bought tickets and found their seats inside. As the lights dimmed and the opening credits rolled, Mateo let himself relax into the darkness of the cinema. It had been years since he had done something as ordinary as watching a film, and he found the simplicity oddly refreshing. Carolina leaned over once or twice to whisper a question about the plot, and Nick chuckled softly in response.

Halfway through the movie, Mateo's eyes wandered across the theater—and froze. Just a few rows ahead, he saw a face he knew too well. Fr. Chris.

The pastoral director sat with a young woman at his side—none other than the same girl from St. Raphael College who had once pleaded with Mateo for help. The two were seated close, too close for a priest and a student, their heads leaning toward each other in a familiarity that spoke more loudly than any words.

Mateo's heart jolted. He shifted in his seat, torn between looking away and staring long enough to confirm what he already knew. The weight of their previous confrontations returned to him in an instant—the secrets, the confessions, and the jealousy. And now, here it was, no longer whispered in confidence but laid bare in public view.

When the movie ended, the crowd funneled into the lobby, voices buzzing with laughter and commentary about the film. Mateo, Nick, and Carolina moved in sync with the stream, but Mateo's focus remained on a specific corner.

Fr. Chris stepped into the light of the lobby, his hand brushing the girl's arm in a gesture too intimate to be mistaken. He looked up—and his eyes locked with Mateo's.

For a moment, the world around them seemed to blur. Mateo stood beside Nick and Carolina, the picture of innocent companionship, while Fr. Chris was unmistakably compromised. His jaw tightened, his eyes narrowing as if the simple fact of being seen by Mateo was an accusation in itself.

Neither spoke. The silence between them carried more weight than any confrontation could. Mateo dipped his head slightly, not in acknowledgment but in restraint, choosing not to expose him further in front of strangers. Yet the damage was done. Fr. Chris knew he had been caught.

As the three friends stepped out into the cool night air, Nick chatted lightly about the film, oblivious to the storm brewing behind Mateo's eyes. Carolina smiled politely, unaware of the silent battle that had just unfolded in the lobby.

But Mateo felt it in his bones: another rift had deepened. Whatever fragile bond he once shared with Fr. Chris was now fractured beyond repair.

Mateo returned to the seminary gates early the next morning, his bag slung across his shoulder, the faint sound of the chapel bells tolling Prime echoing across the compound. The semester break had been long enough to reset his body, but not his mind. The memory of the previous night in the theater still clung to him—the unmistakable look of panic in Fr. Chris's eyes when their gazes met in the lobby.

Inside his room, Mateo carefully unpacked his belongings. Books were arranged in meticulous rows on his desk. His cassock was hung crisply in the wooden wardrobe. The few personal mementos he allowed himself—a rosary and a photograph of his parents—were placed neatly in their usual spots. For Mateo, order was more than a habit; it was a shield.

He sat at the edge of his bed, letting the silence of the seminary surround him. Outside, voices of seminarians returning from their own breaks floated through the hallways, footsteps echoing against the stone floors. Mateo felt a mixture of anticipation and caution. The second semester loomed like an unopened book, its blank pages heavy with the promise of unwritten trials.

A soft knock at his door broke the stillness. It was Nick, cheerful as always, greeting him with a broad smile. "Welcome back, Mateo! The second semester begins, and you look like you're about to face a battlefield."

Mateo smiled faintly. "In some ways, Nick, every semester feels like one."

As they walked together to the refectory, Mateo's mind was elsewhere. He could not erase the image of Fr. Chris in the theater. He knew that eventually, there would be a reckoning—whether silent avoidance or outright confrontation. For now, though, Mateo resolved to bury himself in his duties: the studies, the presidency of the student body, the choir rehearsals, and the endless cycle of responsibilities that demanded his focus.

Still, beneath the calm surface, Mateo sensed the quiet shifting of forces around him. Rumors, ambitions, rivalries—these were not left behind with the old semester. The stone walls of the theology building awaited him, alive and eager.

And with Fr. Chris's secret now exposed, Mateo felt a new shadow had entered his path.

CHAPTER 26

The Unexpected Regency

The day had begun like any other, with the familiar rhythm of seminary life—Lauds in the chapel, breakfast in the refectory, and a quick review of notes before the morning lectures. Mateo, eager to start the new semester with renewed focus, carried himself with the quiet discipline that had earned him respect from many of his peers.

But midway through the morning, a message came: *The Rector wishes to see you in his office immediately.*

Mateo's steps were steady as he walked down the corridor, but his heart carried a weight of unease. He had done nothing wrong—or so he thought. However, the Rector's summons were always a serious matter.

Father Michael sat behind his desk, his face unreadable. "Mateo," he began, his tone calm but distant, "after consultation with some of the formators, we feel it would be good for you to take a six-month leave from seminary formation. What we call *regency*."

The word landed like a stone in Mateo's chest. "Regency?" he repeated, his voice tight. "Why, Father? I don't understand. Have I failed in some area? Is there a problem with my studies, with my duties?"

The Rector folded his hands and leaned back in his chair. "It is not about failure. Sometimes, the seminary discerns that a man needs time outside to gain perspective. To… test his vocation in the world."

Mateo frowned. "But why now? I've just begun my second semester. I have responsibilities here. I've been entrusted with leadership. I—" His voice cracked, but he steadied himself. "I deserve to know the reason."

Father Michael shifted uncomfortably. "It would be better if you spoke with Father Prefect. He may provide more clarity."

The dismissal was firm, and Mateo had no choice but to bow slightly and leave the office, his mind churning.

Father Prefect greeted him with his usual gentleness, seated in the shaded garden where his beloved bonsai trees stood in perfect rows. When Mateo posed the same question, the Prefect sighed.

"Mateo," he said, "I wish I could explain. But the decision is not mine. You must understand—sometimes the ways of formation are not straightforward. The Rector asked me to guide you to another person who might give you what you seek."

"Who?" Mateo asked, his patience thinning.

"Father Chris."

At that name, a spark of realization cut through Mateo's confusion. His stomach tightened, and fragments of memory collided—the theater, the girl's pleading eyes, and Fr. Chris's anger afterward. It was as if a veil had lifted.

He found Father Chris later that afternoon in the choir room, seated at the piano, his fingers idly pressing a melody that never quite formed.

"Father Chris," Mateo said, standing in the doorway, his voice steady but edged with resolve.

The priest looked up, almost startled. "Mateo. Come in."

Mateo stepped inside, letting the heavy wooden door close behind him. "I've been told to take a regency. The Rector gave no reason. Father Prefect gave no reason. And then they sent me to you." His eyes narrowed. "Why, Father? What did you say about me?"

For a moment, silence filled the room except for the faint creak of the piano stool. Fr. Chris's lips pressed into a thin line, his eyes refusing to meet Mateo's.

"Not everything can be said plainly," Fr. Chris muttered at last. "Decisions are made for the good of all."

"No," Mateo said firmly. "This has nothing to do with the good of all. This has to do with you. With what you think you saw. With what you refuse to believe about me."

The accusation hung in the air, heavy and sharp.

Fr. Chris's face hardened. "You don't understand, Mateo. You never will."

Mateo's chest tightened with both anger and sorrow. In that instant, he understood fully: his path had been twisted, not by discernment or divine will, but by human frailty—by jealousy, fear, and betrayal dressed in clerical robes.

He turned toward the door, his voice low but resolute. "If this is your doing, Father, then may God judge between us."

The door closed behind him, leaving the echo of his words to linger in the choir room.

Chapter 27

A Reluctant Departure

Mateo stayed one more night in the seminary. He lingered in the silence of his room long after Compline had ended, staring at the crucifix above his bed, trying to reconcile obedience with the storm that was tearing at his heart.

Obedience. It was the vow whispered into every seminarian's soul since day one, the cornerstone of formation. To obey one's superiors was to obey Christ Himself, the formators being seen as God's chosen representatives. Mateo repeated this teaching to himself like a prayer, but it gave him little comfort.

He would rather not leave. Every corner of the seminary—the chapel where he spent countless hours in prayer, the choir loft that had become his second home, and the lecture halls where he wrestled with philosophy and theology—was tied to his sense of purpose. To walk away now felt like tearing off a part of himself.

Yet, by the following morning, there was no other choice. With quiet hands, he folded his cassock, stacked his books, and carefully packed the personal mementos that had accompanied him through years of struggle. Each item carried a memory, and each memory deepened the sorrow pressing on his chest.

The taxi driver helped him load his modest trunk into the back seat. As the vehicle pulled away from the seminary gates, Mateo's eyes lingered on the building growing smaller behind him. He felt as though he were being exiled from the very place that had been both his battlefield and his sanctuary.

When the driver asked, *"Where to,* sir?" Mateo hesitated. He had no plan, no destination. For a few moments he sat in silence, watching the streets blur past, until he remembered an orphanage in a suburb not far from the city. The name surfaced gently, like a forgotten prayer—St. Dominic's Orphanage.

"Take me there," Mateo finally said.

The orphanage stood humbly at the edge of town, its gates modest, its walls echoing with the faint sound of children's laughter. There, Mateo asked for the director.

Father Julius, a priest with a kind face and weathered hands, welcomed him without hesitation. Listening to Mateo's story, he nodded with quiet understanding.

"You may stay here, Mateo," he said warmly. "Regency is not exile. It is part of formation, though it feels harsh now. But you must inform the Rector where you are. The Church must know where her son resides."

The words offered a fragile comfort. For the first time since leaving the seminary, Mateo felt he was not entirely adrift.

That evening, as he unpacked his trunk in the small room Fr. Julius had assigned him, Mateo reflected on the strange turn of events. He had thought himself alone in this trial, singled out for reasons still hidden. However, he soon discovered that they had also asked Nick, his trusted friend, and four other seminarians to leave on the same day.

Six seminarians. One day.

The seminary corridors buzzed with whispers. *"It has never happened before,"* some said. Mateo could almost hear their disbelief traveling across the walls he had just left behind. The event was marked not as an accident of timing but as a deliberate stroke of decision, its reasoning locked in silence.

In the orphanage, as the children's voices carried faintly through the evening air, Mateo sat at the edge of his bed. He pressed his rosary into his palm and whispered:

"Lord, if this is Your hand, let me see the path. But if this is the hand of men, give me the strength to endure it."

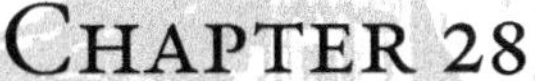

CHAPTER 28

Questions in the Halls

The departure of six seminarians in one day was like a stone thrown into still water. The ripples spread quickly across the seminary grounds, unsettling the calm rhythm of lectures, prayers, and meals. Students whispered in corridors, hushed voices rising and falling with rumors. Some said the six had broken a hidden rule. Others thought it was politics between priests. But no one could point to a clear reason.

Brother Felipe, a senior seminarian and a candidate for the deaconate, could not ignore the unease. He had observed these younger seminarians, and he knew their strengths, their weaknesses, and above all, their dedication. Mateo's sudden removal—without warning, without explanation—struck him as unjust.

During a departmental meeting, Felipe raised the matter directly.

"Reverend Fathers," he said firmly, his voice carrying over the polished oak table, "I must ask: on what grounds were six seminarians dismissed on the same day? One of them, Mateo, was among our most diligent theology students. If there is a matter of discipline, should it not be handled with clarity?"

The room grew tense. Some priests shifted in their seats; others kept their eyes fixed on their papers. The Rector cleared his throat but offered only a vague reply.

"These decisions were necessary for the good of the seminary," he said. "The details need not be discussed further."

Felipe leaned forward. "But Father Rector, with all due respect, how do we justify this to the student body? They are asking questions. Rumors are dangerous in a place like this. Would it not be better to provide the truth, rather than silence?"

Still, no clear answer came. The priests insisted that the decision had been made and was final and binding.

"Obedience must be observed," said Fr. Prefect curtly. "That is all the seminarians need to understand."

But obedience, Felipe knew, did not erase conscience. The whispers in the dormitories only grew louder, the unease more pronounced.

It was not long before word of the dismissals reached the ears of His Eminence, the Cardinal. A man who carried both pastoral warmth and sharp discernment, the Cardinal had always insisted on transparency within his clergy. When the report came—six seminarians, one day, no explanation—his concern deepened.

He summoned the Rector and his staff to the archdiocesan chancery.

"I want to know," the Cardinal said slowly, his eyes scanning the room, "why six men preparing for priesthood were removed without just cause. I want a full account of what transpired in the theology building. These are not faceless numbers. These are souls entrusted to us."

The silence that followed was heavier than stone.

Thus, a special investigation was ordered. For the first time in years, the seminary found itself under scrutiny, its decisions no longer hidden behind cloistered walls. Questions of fairness, transparency, and authority now stood at the center of the storm.

And for Mateo, still adjusting to life at the orphanage, the news of the Cardinal's intervention would soon reach him. The struggle he thought was personal was becoming something larger—a test not only of his vocation but of the integrity of the very institution that had formed him.

CHAPTER 29

The Cardinal's Inquiry

The inquiry began quietly but carried the weight of authority behind it. The Cardinal appointed a small commission of three senior priests—men respected for their impartiality—to conduct interviews with faculty and students alike. What had started as whispers in corridors was now the subject of official scrutiny.

In the theology building, seminarians were summoned one by one into a plain meeting room. A crucifix hung above the doorway, and the scent of incense lingered faintly from morning prayers. But the atmosphere was far from peaceful.

"Tell us what you know," one of the investigators asked Felipe when it was his turn.

Felipe folded his hands on the table. "What I know is this: six seminarians, including Mateo, were told to leave without explanation. I have known most of them myself. None had serious infractions. Some were strong students, devoted to their studies. If there is a reason, it has not been shared with us. And that silence itself is harmful."

The investigators noted his words carefully. They heard similar testimonies from other seminarians, though some were cautious, unwilling to speak openly against the Rector's office. Still, a pattern emerged: no one could point to a legitimate cause for the mass dismissal.

Meanwhile, the seminarians still in residence felt the weight of every question. Some admitted they had seen tensions between Mateo and Fr. Chris. Others hinted at jealousies, though none could say more.

It was during one of these sessions that a brave theology student spoke aloud what many had only whispered.

"Fathers," he said hesitantly, "we all know that Mateo saw something he was not supposed to. He saw Fr. Chris outside… with a woman. And thereafter, things changed. Perhapsthe incidents has something to do with his dismissal?"

The room fell silent. The investigators exchanged glances. At last, they wrote the words down.

Far from the seminary walls, Mateo was trying to build a routine at the orphanage. The laughter of children filled the halls, and Fr. Julius welcomed his presence as a tutor and mentor for the young ones. Yet Mateo's heart was restless. At night, lying on the narrow cot assigned to him, he replayed the moment he left the seminary—his books packed neatly, his room left bare, and the sting of being told to go without a reason.

One afternoon, Nick came to visit, carrying a letter folded tightly in his pocket. His face was tense but hopeful.

"Mateo," he said, handing him the letter, "there's something happening. The Cardinal himself has ordered an investigation. They're asking questions—serious ones. About why we were all told to leave."

Mateo froze. He read the words over and over. His heart surged with a mixture of relief and dread. Relief that someone finally cared enough to search for the truth. Dread because he suspected that truth pointed to Fr. Chris—and if exposed, the fallout would shake the seminary to its core.

He looked at Nick. "Do you think… it will change anything?"

Nick shrugged, though his eyes carried a flicker of hope. "At least they are asking. That is more than we had before."

Mateo folded the letter carefully and slipped it into his breviary. As the bells of the orphanage chapel rang for evening prayer, he whispered to himself: *Lord, if truth is coming into the light, give me the strength to face it.*

For now, the investigation pressed forward. But in the corridors of power, the one name that kept surfacing—whether whispered, hinted, or spoken outright—was Fr. Chris.

And Mateo knew that if the commission pressed hard enough, the facade would crack.

A New Home in Song

The orphanage chapel was small, its white-washed walls glowing golden in the late afternoon sun. Wooden pews lined the room, worn smooth by years of hands resting and knees bowing. Here, Mateo's life found a new rhythm.

Officially, he was now the music teacher of St. Dominic's Orphanage. His students were not seminarians preparing for priesthood but children—some barely able to reach the top of the piano keys, others with voices bright and clear like sparrows at dawn. Alongside them were the caretakers, the "uncles" and the "mothers" who ran the day-to-day life of the home. They, too, joined Mateo's music sessions, laughing at their own off-key attempts, clapping to rhythms, and learning harmonies as if rediscovering something lost in themselves.

Mateo poured himself into the work. Each morning, after prayers and breakfast, he would gather the children in a circle. He taught them hymns for the Sunday Mass, playful rounds for recreation, and solemn pieces for feast days. He introduced them to rhythms on makeshift percussion—wooden spoons, tin cans, anything that could carry a beat. Soon, the walls of the orphanage echoed with music that seemed to rise beyond the chapel roof.

The children adored him. They tugged at his sleeves, begged him for songs before bedtime, and watched in awe whenever he played the guitar. "Tito Mateo," they called him, their voices carrying a tenderness that eased the wounds left by the seminary's rejection.

One evening, after leading the children in song at vespers, Mateo lingered at the piano alone. His fingers moved slowly over the keys, weaving melodies not for competition, nor approval, nor reputation—but for joy, for healing. The notes lifted like prayers into the dusky air.

Fr. Julius, passing by, stopped at the doorway. He listened silently for a while before stepping in. "You belong here, Mateo," he said softly. "Not because you were sent, but because the children have chosen you. They love you as one of their own."

Mateo swallowed hard, his throat tight with emotion. For the first time since leaving the seminary, he felt what it meant to be embraced, not judged.

In the weeks that followed, Mateo became more than just the music teacher. He helped with chores, told stories in the evenings, patched up skinned knees, and offered gentle counsel to children who woke in the night crying for parents they barely remembered. The orphanage family folded him into its heart.

And yet—beneath it all—a quiet unease remained. When the children sang their songs, their voices pure and unburdened, Mateo's heart rejoiced. But when the music ended and silence crept in, his thoughts wandered back to the seminary, to the investigation that loomed, and to the confrontation with Fr. Chris that still burned in his memory.

Still, for now, the orphanage was his refuge. A place where music was not a weapon, nor a contest, nor a mark against him—but a gift, freely given, freely received.

For Mateo, it was the first taste of peace in a long time.

CHAPTER 31

The Song of St. Dominic

The anniversary of St. Dominic's Orphanage was unlike anything Mateo had ever witnessed. By dawn, the courtyard was already alive with the smell of roasted meats, the clatter of pots, and the laughter of children helping to decorate. Garlands of bright paper flowers swayed gently from the eaves, and a makeshift stage had been built beside the chapel.

For weeks, Mateo had prepared the program. The children would open the celebration with a hymn he had taught them—simple, tender, yet full of hope. The uncles and aunties, shy at first, would follow with a rousing number that Mateo had patiently rehearsed with them until even the most hesitant voices found their courage.

When the hour came, the courtyard filled with guests—benefactors, neighbors, parishioners, and clergy. But when the orphanage director, Fr. Julius, announced the guest of honor, a hushed awe fell over the crowd. The Cardinal himself had come. His crimson robes seemed to catch the morning light, and his presence gave the humble celebration the dignity of a cathedral.

The children filed onto the stage, Mateo guiding them with quiet nods. As they sang, their voices carried innocence and joy that touched everyone listening. Some wiped their eyes; others smiled with unguarded warmth. For Mateo, standing just off to the side, it was as though their song lifted the very heart of the orphanage into the heavens.

Then came the uncles and the mothers. Their performance was less polished but filled with laughter and a spirit that charmed the crowd. Even the Cardinal chuckled as one uncle missed his entrance and then recovered with theatrical flair.

When the last note faded, applause filled the courtyard. The Cardinal rose, stepping forward to bless the children, laying his hand on their heads one by one. Then, unexpectedly, he turned to Mateo.

"Young man," the Cardinal said in a firm but kindly voice, "you have given these children a wonderful gift. Music that comes from the heart can heal wounds deeper than words."

Mateo bowed respectfully, unsure how to respond.

After Mass and the communal meal, when the guests began to disperse, the Cardinal sought Fr. Julius. The two priests spoke quietly, their eyes occasionally flicking toward Mateo. Finally, the Cardinal approached him directly.

"Come to my residence tomorrow," he said with a gravity that left no room for refusal. "There are matters we must discuss."

Mateo felt his stomach tighten. He nodded, murmuring, "Yes, Your Eminence."

As the Cardinal departed, escorted by his aides, Mateo stood rooted in place. The children tugged at his sleeves, begging him to join their games, but his thoughts were already elsewhere. He could not shake the certainty that this moment was about the seminary, about the shadow of rumors and dismissal that still haunted him.

That night, as the orphanage settled into silence, Mateo lay awake listening to the faint hum of crickets beyond his window. He should have felt content—the celebration had been a triumph, the children's joy was pure, and the Cardinal himself had praised his work. Yet unease gnawed at him.

Tomorrow, answers might finally come. Or tomorrow, new questions might break open old wounds.

Either way, Mateo knew: the Cardinal's summons could not be taken lightly.

CHAPTER 32

The Cardinal's Offer

The Cardinal's residence stood at the heart of San Agustin, a sprawling old structure with high arched windows and heavy wooden doors polished by years of reverent hands. The guards at the gate, recognizing Mateo's name, ushered him in without hesitation. Inside, the air smelled faintly of old books and candle wax, the kind of scent Mateo had always associated with authority and tradition.

He was led to a sitting room where afternoon light spilled through tall windows onto shelves lined with leather-bound volumes. When the Cardinal entered, not in his ceremonial robes but in a simple cassock, Mateo felt both awe and a sudden, familiar warmth.

"It has been a long time since Santa Monica," the Cardinal said, his voice gentler than the commanding tones heard at the orphanage the day before. He motioned for Mateo to sit. "I still remember our walks in the seminary garden. You had so many questions back then."

Mateo bowed his head, recalling those conversations—the way the Archbishop, now Cardinal, had shaped his thoughts and prayers. "I owe much of my formation to you, Your Eminence," Mateo said quietly.

The Cardinal's eyes studied him. "And yet I find you here, in the orphanage, sent away on what they call 'regency.' Six seminarians dismissed in one day, Mateo. No reason given. No explanation to the community. You understand why I ordered an investigation?"

"Yes, Your Eminence," Mateo answered softly.

"Tell me," the Cardinal leaned forward, "what truly happened in the theology building?"

Mateo spoke slowly, recounting what little he knew—the abrupt dismissal, the confused instructions, and the painful realization that Fr. Chris may have pushed for his leave. He neither accused nor defended, but his words carried the weight of bewilderment and sorrow.

The Cardinal listened without interruption, his face unreadable. When Mateo finished, silence filled the room, broken only by the ticking of the clock in the corner.

Finally, the Cardinal rose, walked to the window, and spoke with measured authority. "What was done to you and the others was unjust. And injustice in the seminary poisons the Church itself. I cannot stand idle while envy and politics wound vocations."

He turned, his eyes piercing yet paternal. "Mateo, I am offering you a way forward. You will continue your theological studies in Rome. I will shoulder everything—tuition, travel, and residence. All of it."

Mateo froze. Rome—the heart of the Church, the dream of countless seminarians. The opportunity both dazzled and terrified him. He looked at the Cardinal, then down at his hands resting on his lap.

"Your Eminence," Mateo said slowly, his voice almost trembling, "this is too great an offer for me to answer lightly. I… I need time. To pray. To think. To be sure that this is truly God's will, not only my own desire."

The Cardinal regarded him for a long moment. Then, a small smile touched his lips, tinged with respect. "You are wise to hesitate. Many would have grasped the offer without pause. Take the time you need, Mateo. But do not delay too long. The Church moves quickly, and so does life."

Mateo bowed deeply. "Thank you, Your Eminence."

"Very well," the Cardinal said, his tone softening. "Rest here at the orphanage. The investigation will proceed. When you are ready to answer, my door is open."

As Mateo left the residence, he felt that the city was strangely heavy, as if it were burdened by his uncertainty. The promise of Rome glimmered like a star on the horizon, yet Mateo's heart whispered with unease: *Was this truly God's path for him, or merely another trial in disguise?*

CHAPTER 33

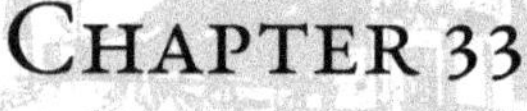

Truth Unveiled

The investigation ordered by the Cardinal moved swiftly, with a gravity that sent ripples of unease through the entire theology department. For weeks, seminarians whispered in corridors, their voices hushed, their glances nervous. Priests who had once carried themselves with untouchable authority now walked with measured steps, as though the very air had shifted.

Testimonies were gathered from seminarians across all levels, including those who had quietly endured the weight of suspicion and politics. Slowly, a clearer picture emerged—and at its center stood Mateo.

It was Rico who first cracked under questioning. His connection to Miss Lolita, long concealed, was uncovered through records, letters, and accounts from seminarians who had noticed his secretive meetings. Rico admitted—though reluctantly—that he had been used as a channel to spread the rumor painting Mateo as a rebel leader, tied to left-wing groups hostile to the government. It was a fabrication, a carefully woven lie meant to tarnish Mateo's name and destroy his vocation.

When pressed further, Rico confessed that Miss Lolita herself had orchestrated much of it, still nursing her obsession and vendetta. The panel of investigators, representing the Cardinal's office, listened in silence as the pieces fit together—how personal grudges had spilled into holy grounds, poisoning lives.

But Rico's exposure was only the beginning.

The name of Fr. Chris surfaced with painful clarity. A group of students from St. Raphael College, emboldened by the inquiry, spoke of inappropriate closeness and favoritism. Among them was the girl who had once wept to Mateo in private. Her testimony was decisive. Though reluctant, she spoke the truth of her relationship with Fr. Chris. The secret was no longer rumor—it became fact under oath.

When confronted, Fr. Chris tried at first to deflect, invoking his pastoral duties and the blurred lines of mentorship. But the evidence, corroborated by students and even staff of the college, was overwhelming. His involvement was undeniable.

And still, the investigation pressed deeper.

Questions reached the rector, the prefect, and the liturgy director. Each was scrutinized not for moral failings, but for the misuse of Mateo's gifts. It became evident that Mateo's multi-faceted talents—his leadership, his music, his organizational skill—had been fought over, like pieces of a prize. Each priest, in his own way, had wanted Mateo's time and energy bent toward his own agenda.

The prefect, with his garden and strict physical regimen, had wanted Mateo's assistance for tasks beyond his seminary formation. The liturgy director, who had long dominated the seminary's ceremonies, grew resentful when Mateo's own compositions and leadership began to outshine him. The rector, while more discreet, had allowed these struggles to persist, perhaps out of weakness, perhaps out of complacency.

The pattern was clear: the internal politics of the seminary had warped the very mission it claimed to uphold.

When the final report was placed before the Cardinal, he sat in silence for a long time, his fingers steepled, his eyes closed as though in prayer.

Then he gave his decision.

"Theology must be purified," he said solemnly. "This house cannot form men of God while it is itself fractured by envy, misuse, and betrayal. Therefore, I order a total restructuring of leadership."

It was swift and merciless:

The rector was relieved of his position and reassigned to a distant parish.

The prefect was transferred to another diocese for retraining.

The liturgy director was dismissed from his post and placed under disciplinary observation.

Fr. Chris, after further deliberation, was suspended from active ministry pending canonical review.

The entire theology department was placed under temporary oversight by a new rector personally chosen by the Cardinal—one with a reputation for fairness, humility, and detachment from the old politics.

The announcement fell like thunder. Seminarians who had once been silenced by fear now exhaled relief. Some priests looked stricken, others quietly resigned. And in the midst of it all, Mateo, though not entirely free of sorrow, felt the tremors of truth finally cracking the walls that had long weighed against him.

But even as justice rolled like a cleansing tide, Mateo's heart remained heavy. He had not sought vengeance, only peace. And yet, as he stood in the chapel that evening, the glow of candles reflecting in his eyes, he could not shake the question that had haunted him from the beginning:

Why must his path to God be strewn with so many battles, even within the very house of God?

Chapter 34

The Last Discernment

The orphanage, with its laughter, its songs, and its quiet moments of prayer, became a sanctuary for Mateo. He was no longer burdened with timetables, reports, or the ever-watchful eyes of the formators. For the first time in years, he felt free to breathe—to simply exist in God's presence without being told how that presence should look.

Still, the questions remained. What was God truly asking of him? Was the priesthood his destiny, or had it been only a path meant to shape him for something else?

Seeking clarity, Mateo withdrew into silence. He asked Fr. Julius for permission to spend ten days in retreat within the orphanage grounds, apart from the noise of duties. A small room was cleared for him near the chapel, and each day he immersed himself in prayer, Scripture, and journaling. He walked the gardens at dawn, sat among the children during meals, and in the evenings knelt in the chapel until the candles burned low.

By the seventh day, clarity began to emerge—not through visions, but through a deep, inner conviction.

Three incidents confirmed what his heart was beginning to tell him.

The first came when a visiting bishop from a neighboring diocese sought him out. Having heard of the investigation's outcome, the bishop invited Mateo to transfer, promising him a new beginning, a clean slate, and the chance to continue toward priesthood elsewhere. Mateo listened politely, but when pressed, he shook his head. "No, Bishop. I cannot. My vocation does not lie there anymore."

The second was a conversation with a Spanish missionary who had come to San Agustin to recruit seminarians for formation in Spain. "In Madrid, you will be given every opportunity," the missionary insisted. "Your gifts will be honored. Your wounds healed." But again, Mateo declined. "Father, I thank you. But I cannot give myself to a path that no longer is mine."

The third and final incident was the hardest.

Miss Lolita appeared at the orphanage one late afternoon, her face pale but determined. She asked to speak with Mateo privately, and against his better judgment, he agreed. Her confession spilled out in torrents: how she had orchestrated the rumors, how she had driven Rico into betrayal, and how every move she made was meant to pull him back to her side.

Tears streaked her face as she fell to her knees. "Mateo, I love you. I have always loved you. Come with me—let us start anew. Be my life partner, and I will devote myself to you for the rest of my life."

Her words pierced him, but not with affection—only with anger, sorrow, and a deep sense of violation. He stared at her, his voice trembling but firm.

"You destroyed my name. You poisoned my vocation. You shattered the path I once walked—all because of your selfishness. I cannot love you. I do not want to see you again. Leave."

Miss Lolita sobbed, but Mateo turned away. For the first time, the weight of her shadow was lifted from him.

When his retreat ended, Mateo emerged not with doubt but with freedom. He knew now, with certainty, that God was not calling him to be a priest.

His years of formation had not been wasted—they had formed his spirit, deepened his faith, and given him strength to stand. But the path ahead was different.

He requested an audience with the Cardinal.

Seated once again in the familiar residence where so many turning points of his life had unfolded, Mateo spoke with calm determination. "Your Eminence," he said, "I have prayed, I have searched, and I have listened. I believe God does not want me to become a priest. My vocation is to live my faith as an ordinary man—serving in whatever ways I can, but free from rules that others use to manipulate. I wish to live with God's blessing, as His son, in freedom."

The Cardinal looked at him long and silently, then rose from his chair. He placed both hands gently on Mateo's shoulders. His voice, though solemn, carried no hint of disappointment.

"Mateo, the Church does not lose you. You remain a son of God, a disciple of Christ. Your freedom is not abandonment—it is fidelity to the truth you have found. I bless you, and I will always support you."

Relief, like cool water, washed over Mateo.

At last, he was free.

Epilogue

Mateo got married, was blessed with three beautiful children, and later migrated to another country to begin life anew with his family. Far from the walls of the seminary, far from the intrigues and manipulations of the past, he embraced a life of ordinary joys: raising his children, nurturing his marriage, and building a home grounded in love and faith.

He never forgot the seminary—the trials, the betrayals, the friendships, the music, and the countless lessons about God and about human frailty. But he carried them not as chains but rather as stones that paved his new road forward.

Mateo's story reminds us that life is rarely a straight path. Sometimes what feels like defeat is, in truth, the beginning of freedom. The seminary shaped him, tested him, and nearly broke him. Yet in walking away, he found what God had quietly prepared all along: a life of love, a family to call his own, and the courage to be true to himself.

His journey is not just about betrayal or survival, but about redemption—about learning that God's will is not always what others demand of us, but what quietly stirs in our own hearts. Mateo chose not to live under shadows but in light. He chose family, truth, and love. And in that choice, he found peace.

The story of Mateo is the story of every soul who has wrestled with expectations, who has stumbled under the weight of false judgments, yet discovered freedom in living authentically. It is a reminder that sometimes, the greatest calling is not to the altar, but to the everyday holiness of a life lived with integrity and love.

In the end, Mateo was not defeated. He was never broken. He was simply free.

"And so, with his family beside him and faith still burning quietly in his heart, Mateo stepped into the rest of his life—not as a priest, not as a victim, but as a man finally free."

www.ingramcontent.com/pod-product-compliance
Lightning Source LLC
Chambersburg PA
CBHW071013180726
48291CB00004B/1439